Fire and Ice

* why were the parents so irresponsible to have so many kids?
* what was the point of the chapter headings in different languages
* why was the book set in a different universe which there had no relevance to the book.
* a good first book of an author who will market into a 'novel' author.)
* why did it take the father so long to die & why was he in hospital for so many years!

Fire and Ice

Elizabeth E. Burdon

Astraea Publications

ISBN-13: 978-1548374471

ISBN-10: 1548374474

Editing by C. Orme.

Cover Image by C. Thornton redbubble.com/people/toastedghost

Printed and bound in UK

First printing November 2017

Published by Astraea Publications info@astraeapublications.co.uk

www.ElizabethEBurdon.com

Instagram and Twitter @eeburdon

www.facebook.com/elizabetheburdon

For Bethany, Lara and Melissa. Don't underestimate the importance of friends, a gift which so many take for granted.

Note on the place where I set my stories

Far away, there is a parallel universe which goes by the name of Nigra Terra. This universe is very multicultural. Some areas of it are full of magic, and some aren't so different from our world.

In Nigra Terra, there is a planet named Somnium. Somnium has many countries within it, one of which is Larenia. Most of Larenia has magic, but there are two counties, called Lilidell and Rosamontis, which are what we would call normal. Oldgate, in West Golding, in Lilidell is where this story is set.

What the people of Earth do not know and refuse to acknowledge, is that Nigra Terra is not so hard to get to from here. One has only to believe it, and it is just over the horizon, behind the clouds. The people of Nigra Terra know this, and they sometimes travel between our two worlds as tourists, studying our culture as we would theirs. The non-magical ones are no different from us, so their presence goes unnoticed. To us, they are just another stranger in the street.

Enjoy the novel. Lizzy Burdon.

Contents

Part I

The sunshine before the storm

Chapter 1

Una noia anomenada Januari

A girl called Januari - Catalan

Jack and Summer Winters' first child was named Januari Snow Winters. She was born on 20th January. She was a very good baby. She didn't cry much, and was very cheerful.

For a short time, it was just Januari and her parents. However, she was very young at this point in her life, and it is that point that is too early for her to remember.

When she was one, her eldest sister was born. This child was named Februari Blanche Winters. Februari looked up to her sister with fierce admiration, trying to do everything she did.

Nothing much changed throughout their lives. Februari was always determined to help her sister, as Januari was her favourite person in the whole world. The two sisters were always close to one another.

Januari spoke her first word at the age of 11 months. The word was 'Friend'. Februari spoke her first word at 13 months. This word was 'Jannie' which didn't surprise anyone.

Januari's hair was a soft but distinct brown. It was also thick and wavy. Her eyes were an intense brown, and she had a very sweet smile that lit up her whole face. Or so people say, anyway. They still say it now, but I disagree.

Januari started walking at the age of one. Februari started a little later at 13 months, and the first thing she did was to walk over to where Januari was.

Januari was three when her next sister, March Hope Winters, was born. When Januari learned to read, she picked up the fairytale book, and read a story to March. March loved stories, and would laugh and clap her hands whenever someone brought one into the room to read to her. 'Story' was her first word when she got to that stage.

As she got older, March started to make up her own stories. She decided at the age of six that she wanted to be an author, and this remained her ambition throughout her life.

Januari proved herself to be very helpful to Summer and Jack when they were looking after her younger sisters. She was always ready to distract one of her sisters, while her parents were occupied with the other. If she was distracting Februari, she'd start up a game to play with her, just those two. If she was distracting March, she'd tell her a story. When she was four, she made up a song which she sang to her sisters to help them go to sleep. Soon, she was singing to them every night, and they couldn't or wouldn't settle down to sleep unless they were drifting off to the sound of Januari singing.

"Be calm, unwind, as you lie in my arms this night.

Relax, keep still, as you let sleep carry you away-ay-ay,

Let it go...all that stress and worry, and all that makes you nervous

Sleep in peace, for you are loved.

Sleep in peace for you are loved,

Sleep, darling, sleep. Dream happy dreams..."

It was a very simple melody, and the words quite repetitive, but it worked effectively as a lullaby, definitely living up to its purpose.

When Januari was four, April was born. April Raina Winters was very different from her sisters. She cried so much more often than they had. She was very nervous, and her feelings were fragile... she got upset more easily. She was very quiet, and very shy. When she was happy, she had a very small, subtle little smile, which everyone loved to see on her face.

Januari knew exactly what April needed: she needed people to be there for her, but she needed to learn to be independent as well. Januari took it upon herself to make sure April got an equal balance of these things.

Summer, Jack and Januari always encouraged April to smile. They would often go on days out, which April loved. Visits to farms and picnics in the park, shopping trips and long walks, trips to the leisure centre and days at the seaside, and visits to theme parks, though they'd only go on the small children's rides.

Their home – Oldgate in Lilidell – couldn't have been more conveniently placed for their days out. If they drove north for half an hour, they'd be at the beach. Golden sand and crystal clear waters. The sea at Lilidell Beach was a beautiful shade of blue, and they all loved frolicking amongst the waves, especially Januari.

If they drove east for half an hour, they'd reach the huge, lush green valleys, and the vast, towering mountains. They loved to climb mountains. Summer would take March and April up the path which they could steer April's pram up, and Jack would take Januari and Februari up the more adventurous path. They would meet at the summit, then head back down the main path together.

If they drove south-east for half an hour, they'd reach Oppidum Lilia – the colossal capital city of Lilidell. They could soak in the city environment, hearing many, many different languages all around them. There were all kinds of shops, and the big Southgate shopping centre. There was so much to do, and they never tired of visiting Oppidum Lilia.

When Januari was five, a fifth child was born. She was May Blossom Winters. She laughed constantly, such a cheerful baby. She would babble happily all day, and seemed to have a permanent smile on her face. Everyone loved May, and always she would smile and wave at people and clap her hands.

However, when May got upset, you knew about it. It was a rare occurrence, but she always was a drama queen. As she got older, she ended up saying a lot of things she didn't mean when she was upset. She knew this, and always gave her sincerest apologies to anyone she'd hurt afterwards.

When Januari went to school, she loved it. The teacher was called Mr Mills. She was a very quick learner with a passion for learning. As a result of this, she and her friends were the four best students in the class. Februari followed in Januari's footsteps, and with a little help from Januari, was just as successful in her first year at school.

After a while, people didn't acknowledge Januari quite as much for her hard work. They got used to the fact that that was what was normal for her. Hard work didn't come naturally to her, but the willingness to work did, and that was what kept her going.

You might be wondering, by this point in the story, who I am and what my part is in all of this. How do I know so much about the Winters family – am I a stalker or something?

Back then, my life was relatively normal, and I am glad to tell of it. I was just a little girl, blissfully unaware of what tragic event would strike my family in a few years' time, and what it would mean for me. Completely oblivious to what the future held for me, I was a happy child – there always seems to be sunshine before a storm.

Little did I know what dark times were ahead of me. Hard times indeed, though life is tolerable, me being who I am.

Sometimes I look back at pictures of me as a child, and smile sadly. I look at my face... such youthful innocence, not a care in the world. My whole face lit up with that smile which so many people praise, but to me, it just looks like a person smiling.

I suppose that in itself is a beautiful thing – a smile. One that reaches the eyes, proof that someone is happy on the inside. Now it is a rare, precious thing. Often, when I smile, it's a strained one. Happy, but not completely happy. You'd be surprised how often it's that kind of smile you're seeing, not a real smile.

I don't smile that carefree smile any more, simply because I'm not carefree. There is plenty to worry about, but also plenty to be glad for. I am content with my everyday life. Yes, it's not ideal, but then again, no one's life is perfect. It's enough for me.

To the first-time reader of this story, I'm babbling a load of complete and utter nonsense. No one knows where their story will end, but mine seems to have been completely mapped out for me already.

No travelling the world, and certainly no falling in love. Just hard work. Though it will probably end happily enough.

Things might pick up a bit in my mid-thirties somewhere, but there still won't be any of the things I used to dream about as a little girl. No travelling the world because there's no money to travel and no transport either.

My story won't be a love story because I have no social life. Admit it – no one would go falling in love with someone who can't spend any time with them, and who isn't going to be able to leave home until their mid-thirties. It just doesn't work that way, but life goes on and I'm not complaining. It's just the way things are, and the choice is to like it or lump it. So I like it.

I'm perfectly happy the way I am, but we're only in chapter one, and this will probably be one of the happiest bits of my story. There's no telling where my life will go, but I think I can take a pretty good guess.

In the part of the story you're reading, I was just a child. A child like any other, an innocent child, a happy child, and my name was the only part of me that stood out. My name is Januari.

Chapter 2
一个幸福的童年
A happy childhood - Chinese

When I was seven, June and July were born. June Goldie Winters and July Sandra Winters were twins. They were very pretty babies, but they didn't bathe in the attention like May did.

They preferred to be in a room on their own, just the two of them. June's first word was 'July' and July's first word was 'June.' They were very different, even as babies, but people say opposites get on very well, and my younger sisters were living proof of this.

All through primary school, I'd had a group of friends – Jemima Nelson, Victoria Rogers and Genevieve Wilkinson. Their parents were good friends of my parents. We always made up stories and just had fun. We liked to talk about our futures.

Victoria wanted to go to university in the Somnian Republic (SR) and study languages, then be a professional translator. Genevieve wanted to be an astrophysicist. Jemima wanted to be an artist. I wanted to find true love, and travel the world. I wanted to see everywhere – Leonia, Natura, the SR, Citania, the Wise Isles, Mysteria...

Leonia, in all its golden glory, all the sights to see in Oppidum Leo like the Gloria Tower, and the mountains...

In Natura I'd go to Oppidum Natura, and I'd see the huge cathedral there. I'd go to the forests, and then to the beach, where I'd sit on the soft, white sand and gaze out across the vast ocean, the sun dazzlingly bright, sparkling on the crystal clear water.

I imagined the Somnian Republic... I didn't know much about it but I'd heard people talking about trips there... the beach, Oppidum Somnia, swimming with dolphins... and it sounded amazing.

Citania, where I could soak in the intense heat of the city in summer, and see all that there was to see there.

In the Wise Isles... well, I'd seen pictures of the coast there, and everything about it looked incredible.

I wanted to go to Mysteria, to climb the mountains there, and just to experience something different.

Oh, somebody stop me or I'll go on talking forever! I wanted to go everywhere... I just wanted to leave the country, but some dreams just sound like that – dreams. Even if you've made specific plans to do something, it doesn't feel real. And it won't be.

I had a complete and fierce faith that all my friends would achieve their dreams. All three of them were very intelligent, and we fitted together like jigsaw pieces. With some people it was just like that. We went through everything together, and they were always there for me.

Jemima Nelson had straight, black hair, and dark olive green eyes. She was also very tall. As there was no uniform at Oldgate Junior and Infant School, we could wear whatever clothes we liked. Jemima liked to wear plain jeans and patterned tops. She had a flowery one, and a checked one, and a stripy one...

She loved art, and she was incredible at it as well. You never needed to ask who the artist of the best piece of work in the class was, because it was always

Jemima. She spent most of her spare time doing some form of art.

Her crowning achievement was her bedroom. Her parents had left the walls white, and she'd painted them. She'd painted herself, and her family and her easel and paint pot. She'd also painted us – Genevieve, Victoria and me. She'd painted all of our four names as well, in a beautiful font. She said the fonts were actually word processor fonts and she was just copying the ones she thought were most like us.

Jemima

Januari

Victoria

Genevieve

There was much more as well... just whatever was on her mind at that moment. One entire wall was a sunset beach. There was the sun on the sea, and dark palm trees and the sand and stars were beginning to appear and no one was there. It was based on her very own adaptation of a poem I wrote:

The Sunset on the Sparkling Sea

By Januari Winters

The golden sand soft on my feet,
The sound of the waves, gentle on the shore,
As the red sun bleeds into the fading pink sky,
The sunset on the sparkling sea.

The ocean contains wonders beyond my comprehension,
So beautiful and yet so terrible,
Green and blue, a monster just sleeping,
The sunset on the sparkling sea.

The cliffs loom high above me,
A fierce beast waiting to strike,
Yet even they surrender to the ocean deep,
The sunset on the sparkling sea.

The sun no longer burns the soft sand,
As day slowly fades into night,
A dangerous red, which many avoid,
The sunset on the sparkling sea.

Time is its only enemy,
The cogs which never cease to turn,
It really is a mysterious thing,
The sunset on the sparkling sea...

It was nothing special really, 'just another of Januari's fantasies,' but Jemima loved that poem, so she turned it into a work of art. There was her sunset beach on one wall, the pictures of people she knew on another, and lots of fairytale characters in a fairytale kingdom on another. The fourth wall, she split into four panels and painted our dreams.

In the first panel, she just did splodges of paint in lots of different colours. In the second, she painted Space – the sun, the moon, the stars, the solar system, black holes... it was an amazing piece of art. In the third panel, she painted a love heart and she painted lots of sights to see from around the world. In the fourth panel, she painted an array of flags. I wouldn't be surprised if she had every country's flag on there.

I always loved going into Jemima's bedroom. I always sighed in wonder when I saw her walls. It was like each time I left, I forgot just how spectacular it was. The ceiling was painted midnight blue, with some luminous stars stuck to it, and she had a wooden floor with a rug on it. It was wise not to have a carpet in Jemima's room, because she'd have covered it in messy stains within a day.

I miss going round to Jemima's house... I haven't seen that bedroom in years now. I won't give too much away. I really must stop *babbling* so. It's a habit of mine. I am useless at keeping my own secrets, because I just babble and say too much and give the whole thing away. I can keep other people's secrets fine, though. Which is kind of necessary when you have 11 sisters. Oh, I'm doing it again. I'm sorry, where was I? Oh yes... my friends. I do miss them.

Victoria Rogers is a linguist. Her grasp of languages is quite astounding. We always used to practise speaking other languages together. We both loved languages. Victoria has short curly light blonde hair and light blue eyes. She is quite small, like me.

Victoria is always nice to everyone she meets. She's very polite, very intelligent, very mature... the perfect pupil, in other words. We were all polite and mature, but I'd say Victoria was the most. She had her own sense of style, very quirky and different. We were all like that. None of us really cared about colour schemes or fashion – we just chose clothes we liked to suit ourselves. We were all very similar, but very different at the same time.

Victoria liked to wear a bright orange t-shirt and her scruffy jeans. She said orange was her favourite colour because it was individual and unique. We were all for being individual and unique… but now I just wish I could have lived a normal life instead of striving to stand out in a crowd. I know it's wrong to wish that… there are many people who are worse off and what I do have is a blessing to me… I don't know what to say. Oh, I need to stop talking now. I'm saying too much again.

Genevieve Wilkinson has long straight ginger hair – which she usually tied back into a ponytail, and she wore glasses. She was short-sighted. She was so much happier when she had her glasses because it meant she could see long distances, and *that* meant she could see the night sky better. Once, she got a telescope for her birthday, and you could find her, every clear night after that, on the balcony outside gazing awestruck at the night sky through her telescope.

There was something about the night sky which fascinated us all. I didn't understand how most people just didn't notice what an amazing thing the night sky was. It was the most beautiful thing I'd ever seen. I wished people would see the night sky for the celestial beauty that it was. Funny thing to wish for, really, considering… certain things.

I never really blamed Genevieve for wanting to be an astrophysicist. It would be a dream job just to study space every day. I'm sure she'll get there as well. She will definitely be an astrophysicist one day. I have always had complete confidence that my friends will achieve their ambitions.

Now, when I look up at the night sky, I think of Genevieve, and how she's doing. Then I think of Jemima and Victoria. I do miss them.

Genevieve never really bothered about what she was wearing. She just grabbed any old thing from her wardrobe, got dressed as quickly as she could, and continued with whatever science stuff she was doing.

Sometimes the combination of what she was wearing made us smile and shake our heads, but we understood and we were in complete sympathy with her obsession as well. We all understood each other, and we got along fine. We never really fell out. If one of us got crabby with the others, we'd understand and if one of us was upset we knew exactly what to do – what she needed to make her feel better.

It was such a good feeling knowing that you always had your three friends there for you. We never really needed to stand up for each other... we were all very independent; we still are.

We knew each other right from reception to this day. At the point in the story you are at, I was eight. So that's four years we'd known each other already. I'd say that Februari knew me best, then Jemima, Victoria and Genevieve.

Even then, Februari was always there for me as well. I can't even start to say how much Februari means to me. She was there for me when I had no one... which, of course, you don't know about yet.

Februari had her own friends at school, but at home, we'd spend all our time together. Almost never alone, but together nonetheless. I had half an hour or so alone in the evenings to recharge with no one else there, not even Februari.

That was enough, though. Well, it had to be, really. I was thankful for it. Now I don't even get that. Nowadays, I'm lucky if I get two minutes, but I'm not even going to get started on that.

Most of the time at home was spent keeping my sisters entertained. Back then, it wasn't much of a job. There were only six of them. June and July could keep themselves entertained, as could May. Februari stayed with me, and Mum and Father looked after April, so we just sat with March and read endless stories.

I wish I had more time to read now, but it isn't really possible. I don't mind too much – there's plenty to distract me.

So there you have it – the blissful, happy part of my childhood, before it all changed. I'm not going to say it went wrong - we get along fine, and I do my best, but it certainly changed, as you will soon find out...

Chapter 3

Tragedie Rammer

Tragedy Strikes – Danish

For a while before it happened, Father had been short of breath, with a cough. However, none of us could have predicted what was to happen next. We thought it was just a cold. Everyone gets colds, and they pass.

It soon became apparent that this was more than just a cold. My father became tired more frequently, his cough got worse, and he experienced pain in his chest. He lost quite a bit of weight, and he wasn't as hungry as he normally was. By this point, we knew we had to take it to the doctor.

That was the day my father was diagnosed with lung cancer.

The doctors said they couldn't possibly determine at this point whether or not it would be terminal. That was probably the worst part – not knowing what the outcome would be.

Mum started acting differently then. Up until the diagnosis, she'd been the best mum in the world. Always cheerful, made you feel better... she was wonderful.

Father was diagnosed just after their eighth child had been born. She was named Augusta Sunshine Winters. We could all have done with a bit of sunshine then. It was a dark time. I helped Mum with Augusta, because she didn't always have the energy to give Augusta the same care she'd given to my sisters and me.

Whenever she and Father slept through their alarm for 5:30 am, I would get up and sort Augusta out for them.

I called my parents Mum and Father. Mum was just... Mum, she was your average mum, and we loved her. Father... just seemed more like a 'Father' than a 'Dad.' It wasn't because I was being formal... just old-fashioned. I liked to be traditional.

My mother was Summer Isabelle Winters, and she worked in a big office. It was quite stressful for her, but this didn't show until after Father was diagnosed, and she was more fragile, like April. April was the one who needed her parents the most. The rest of us had each other, and Augusta was just a baby. Mum was so good with my sisters, and she was their *Mum*.

My father was Jack Erasmus Winters. Father was a vicar. We used to go to church every Sunday. I endeavour to get us there now, but the services aren't the same and we can't always manage to get there. Our whole family are Christians. It helped keep me sane... praying does kind of make you feel more peaceful. Once, when I was praying, I thought I heard a voice answer me. It said, "Don't worry, Januari. You will have your happy ending. I have something special in line for you."

Now I'm not sure whether I imagined it or whether it was taking the mick, because there's no way I could have 'something special' waiting just around the next bend. Yeah, right. Definitely. It's not like there's no possibility of any of my dreams coming true or my whole life is on a set path until my mid-thirties or anything. I'm definitely going to live a life filled with sunshine and rainbows. Yay, happiness. Unicorns! Sunshine! Oh, I think I said sunshine twice.

Nonetheless, I don't really think about that because I probably imagined it to make myself feel better. I'm just not buying it, and I'm not feeling overly optimistic at the moment.

Either way, it doesn't directly affect my life now. I don't particularly feel as if anything life-changing is going to happen, so I just go about my business as usual.

It was quite hard telling my friends that Father had been diagnosed with lung cancer, but they were very understanding and made me feel miles better. As they always do.

I just wanted to remember all the happy times, when I was little. I know everything's changed now, and it will never be like that again. It was so perfect before Father got ill, before Mum got depressed, before it all changed. Like the sunshine before the storm. I know that once something's changed forever, there's no changing it back, but still I hope that one day, the storm will pass. Maybe not as sunny as it used to be, but still an improvement.

Sometimes I just feel like bursting out crying because I know that we'll never be that happy family untouched by sorrow again, but life goes on, and I can't afford to waste time... it's a valuable thing. Just as the cogs in the clock never stop turning, I just keep on going no matter what happens. Keeping my eyes on the road. Driving at a fixed pace, not too fast or too slow.

Once Father was diagnosed with cancer, it put a stop to our days out. Most of the time, Father was just too tired. He was in much better health than other cancer patients, and had a better chance of survival. The doctors said that even if he did die, he'd live for longer than most lung cancer patients. I wasn't so sure this was a good thing.

So there were no more days out, but we did have some pretty good nights in. We played board games, we watched films... we had good fun.

Whenever I helped my parents with my sisters, Mum would say, "Thank you, Januari. You're a star... and don't you ever forget that."

I would always smile and tell her it was the least I could do. She always smiled back and said she loved me.

Sometimes, the best thing I could do was to stay out of their way, so during those times, I'd go round to one of my friends' houses, usually Jemima's. I'd go round to Jemima's with Victoria and Genevieve and sit in her bedroom. There was plenty to do, and we'd always have lots of fun.

When Father was first diagnosed, I was nine. Februari was eight, March was six, April was five, May was four, June and July were two and Augusta was just newborn.

During that year when Father was ill, but still at home, things were different. I had to help out a lot more. Mum was under more pressure from her job, but Father always made her feel better. My parents' love for each other was truly a beautiful thing, and everyone could see it.

They met at high school, but until Year 10, they didn't even notice each other. The other one was just another kid in their year, a stranger, but in Year 10, they started noticing each other more.

They talked a bit, and slowly but surely developed a friendship.

All the way to the end of high school, that was all it was – friendship. They went to the same college and that was when they started going out. They then went to the same university and they became closer still.

When Summer left college, she shut out her only other friend – Amanda Thatcher - saying she only needed Jack. We still have Amanda's mobile number somewhere, but she doesn't have our home number, or Summer's mobile. No way of contacting us.

Summer's older sister – Elise – was killed in a car crash when Summer was 19. Summer and Elise had been very close as sisters, always telling each other everything. Much like Februari and myself, and June and July. Summer was heartbroken, and as she was away from home at university at the time, Jack was all the comfort she had. He knew exactly how much her sister had meant to her.

They were married when they were in their early twenties, and Summer said it was the happiest day of her life. To stand there in a long, white dress, with the one she loved next to her, promising to love her forever and they've stood by each other ever since. Jack was everything to Summer.

I was their first child, born when Summer was 25. If Elise had still been alive, she would have been my aunt. Mum said Elise would have loved me, and that I reminded her of Elise sometimes.

I sometimes think about how life would have been different if Elise were still alive. It would certainly have affected us more than it should, as she could have helped me with my... situation. She could really have helped the family, in so many ways. Mum used to tell us about her. She sounds to have been a wonderful sister to my mother... I hope my sisters think about me like that.

I want to be the best I can possibly be to my sisters. I want them to lead as normal a life as possible.

I asked Mum what happened with her and Amanda once, curious as to why the friendship just ended.

At first, she just shook her head and sighed, but I pressed her further and then she started talking.

"It was a long time ago, Januari. It wasn't just Amanda, all my friends... I just shut them all out. Stopped being friends with them. I spent all my time with your father, and I didn't spend any time with them at all any more. Amanda confronted me about it, but I told her I didn't need her any more. I was stupid, and I shouldn't have, and... now she couldn't contact us if she wanted to. There were so many others... even Loveday, who I've known since I was five."

"Why don't you contact her?"

"I don't think she'd ever forgive me for what I did. She probably wouldn't want to see me, Jannie."

One of the things that helped me as things got harder was my books. The characters in stories were my role models, my inspiration. Father had always encouraged me to read, and I remembered countless times when as a little girl, he'd sat with me on the sofa, and helped me to learn to read. I didn't know where I'd be without my father.

I wanted to be independent and strong like Elizabeth Bennet. Hesperus Abendstern and Astra Lagos taught me that you can find happiness in the end, even if it takes a long time to find it. Jane Eyre had already taught me that plain didn't have to be boring. Odysseus taught me that you can survive even with the slimmest chances. Rosanna Reynolds taught me that anyone can be anything. Caroline Black and Philip Raymond taught me that even when people are really different to you, sometimes they are the person you can trust the most. Romeo and Juliet taught me that true love can be found in the most unlikely places.

I learnt valuable lessons from every book I read. The fictional characters taught me to be brave, strong, independent, hard-working and open-minded and to never give up on my dreams... I suppose the hope was there the whole way through, but it just got buried amongst things I considered more important. It has always been that I would do anything for the ones I love. Which is why my family's welfare has always been of utmost importance to me.

I know Father must have felt absolutely awful... imagine being ill, and not knowing if you would survive. Imagine being torn from the ones you love. Or causing them pain, but not being able to do anything about it. Little did I know that one day I'd know exactly how it felt to hurt someone I loved, but not be able to do anything about it... and Mum... I knew it was a thousand times worse for her than it was for my sisters and me. She'd already had her sister taken from her suddenly, and my father had been her only comfort. He'd helped her get through it. He'd always been there for her. Now she was afraid she was going to lose him too. He could be ripped from her suddenly, just like Elise was.

She wouldn't have her true love to make her feel better... only her daughters... and we still had lots of growing up to do. She couldn't have a mature conversation with any of us, and she'd let her friend go a long time before this.

Even looking at us would just remind her of what she'd lost, like a stab of pain in her already broken heart... but that might not happen. All we can do is hope, but hope is a powerful thing. Like a flame that won't go out, a part of someone that they will always keep with them. Hope is something pretty special, and that's why I never let it go. It's one of the things gives me my fieriness, along with my determination and my independence.

No one's insults ever bothered me, because I never cared what other people thought as long as I was doing the right thing for myself.

I always envied my parents the love they had for one another, and still I look upon their relationship with wistful eyes, because I know it's impossible for me to find true love now. Even if I did fall in love, the other person would never feel the same way.

It is difficult to explain my situation... but I will explain it, nevertheless, in the next chapter.

My mum used to tell me stories about herself and Elise. It sounds as if their childhood was very different from ours. She told stories of them in summertime, wearing floral dresses and just lying in the grass in the park, talking. She told stories of them in autumn, wearing waterproof coats and wellies, kicking the fiery leaves, laughing and in the winter, snuggled up together by the fire, drinking mugs of hot chocolate. Stories of the springtime, going to see the lambs in the fields. They would go in the evenings, and watch the sun setting over the hills. It sounded as if they did everything together. My sisters and I do those things too, and special memories like that... I want that to be what my sisters remember when they think of their childhood. I want them to have everything I can give them, and if I have to, I will go further than it takes.

Chapter 4

Dit Misschien een uitdaging

This may be a challenge - Dutch

A year after he was diagnosed, my father was taken to stay in hospital. He was still allowed monthly visits home, but we spent those precious days – well – at home. He would spend the day with my sisters and me, and the evenings with Mum. He would go back to hospital in the morning. We visited him in hospital as often as we could.

We visited him there for the first time a day after he was taken into hospital. I remember it felt strange walking into the hospital. My family and I stayed close together, feeling very small in this big hospital where everything was hospital-ly kind of colours like white and pale green and blue.

A lady at the desk talked to Mum for a bit, and then she led us along endless corridors until she pushed open a door, and we went into the ward. It was full of people in beds, and one of them was my father. We ran over to him.

"Father!" I called.

He smiled warmly when he saw us, "hello, my darlings."

June and July scrambled onto his bed and July threw her arms around him. He held her close and said "I was wondering when I'd see you," he looked around at us all, his eyes lingering on Mum, "Oh, I can't believe this is all really happening."

"We miss you, Father," I said, "do you know if you'll be able to come home?"

"I don't know, Januari, I'm sorry, but how've you been, all of you?"

It didn't feel like long until we had to go, so we all said unwilling goodbyes and headed home. I went up to see Mum that evening, worried about her.

"Mum?" I heard no reply, so I opened the door and went in to find her sat on her bed, crying. "Oh, Mum," I said sympathetically. I went over and sat down next to her.

"Oh, Januari," she sobbed, "I'm just so worried about him."

"He'll be all right," I replied, "he has to be all right."

"I hope so. Falling in love just seems to cause pain, Januari. You should avoid it, if you can. We'll stay with him no matter what happens, but things might be harder from now on."

From then on, I could see her becoming more distant from everything, even us. Just slowly fading; that happy glow she always used to have just dying a little more every day, and there was nothing I could do to stop it or bring it back. Mum's words of advice stuck with me from then on. Avoid falling in love. It just causes pain.

When Father was taken into hospital, it was the final straw for my mother. She just broke down. She couldn't do it any more. At that point, there were eight children to look after and she couldn't cope. My heart melted for her.

So, the evident thing to do was to step up. To care for my sisters, to do for them what a mother usually did for them. To be there for them, to do everything I could to help them lead a normal life, to sacrifice my future and my dreams for their sake and that was exactly what I did.

I was ten years old at the time and I've looked after my sisters ever since. Back then, I was in my last year of primary school. Mum started giving me some money once a week to organise food for us. It might astonish you. I was only a child, after all, but I can, perhaps, pride myself on my readiness to take on a challenge.

The first night she hadn't eaten with us, I'd gone upstairs to ask her about it. I'd knocked on her door and gone in.

"Mum? Aren't you coming for tea? I made macaroni cheese all by myself." (It had seemed like a huge achievement at the time)

"What? Oh... that sounds lovely, darling. No, it's all right, you girls eat without me. I don't really feel like..."

"Okay."

So then I went downstairs and returned a second later with Mum's food on a tray. It was like that a lot from then on.

I went to the supermarket once a week to get food. I'd do simple cooking – like fish pie, macaroni cheese, beans on toast... that was the kind of meal I could make. I could also make soup, and sometimes I'd get us instant meals, like Nippy Noodles or something. We had takeaway at least once a week, usually on a Friday. I planned out the meals for the week.

We all had school dinners, because it was easier, and Mum simply paid online for our school meals, so that was one less job for me.

Februari seemed to think that Mum had completely abandoned us. The way Februari saw it, Mum had forgotten our existence, but I was sure that wasn't true. Mum did love us. She just wasn't in a fit state to look after us. I was sure of it. Februari kept saying I only believed that because I wanted it to be true. It was true that she didn't really pay much attention to us. We hardly ever saw her any more. I tried to make her happy too, but it didn't seem to be any use. However, I was sure that Mum did care about us. She just found things hard, that was all. I was determined for this to be true.

When I had to get June, July and Augusta registered for nursery, I struggled to find a time to go. I didn't want to leave the others with Februari, and it would be too late by the time they were all in bed.

The Sparkling Waters Nursery in Oldgate was open from 7:30am until 5:30pm, and you could take children there for as much or little time as you wanted. It was run by Felicity Jones and her daughter Oriana (Ani) who was 18 at that point, just starting to help Felicity run the nursery. She never needed to think about her future, because all she wanted was to work in the nursery. When Felicity retired, it would belong to her. The Jones family had always run the Sparkling Waters Nursery.

I thought it would be best to take the little ones in the morning before school, and pick them up as soon as I could afterwards.

I eventually decided to go to register them in the evening, just before closing time. Mum would be back then, so I wouldn't be leaving them home alone. I went to the nursery at around 5:00.

I knocked and entered, looking distinctly little-girly. My long hair was in plaits and I was wearing a pale purple dress.

"Hello?" I called out nervously.

A young woman came up to me, smiling. "Hey, kid. What can we do for ya?"

"I was wondering if there were any places going spare... for three of my sisters?"

"Yeah, probably. Where's your mum or dad?"

"At home," I glanced at my feet glumly as I spoke.

"So you're here on your own? Why?" she pressed further.

"That's enough, Ani!" The woman who'd spoken looked to be in her mid-fifties. The younger woman – Ani – scowled and backed down.

"Sorry," she muttered. The older woman smiled brightly.

"Hello, poppet. I'm Felicity Jones and this is my daughter Oriana. What was it you were here about?"

"She already said – she wants to know if there are any spaces for her three sisters," said Ani.

"Let the poor girl speak for herself, Ani. What's your name, little girl?"

"Januari Winters."

"And how old are you, Januari?"

"Ten."

"And I'll need to take your sisters' names and ages."

"June Winters is three. July Winters is also three. Augusta Winters is one."

At this point Ani interrupted again: "so we can definitely take her sisters, can't we, Mum? That'll be fine."

"Yes... of course," she frowned at Ani, "and Januari... why are you here on your own?"

"It's not something I want to discuss," I said firmly.

"Wow, feisty little thing, aren't you? Very independent for your age," Ani cut in.

"I'm not sure if you meant that as a compliment, but thank you."

"Very mature, too. I think we're going to get along well, Januari Winters," she said, grinning. I smiled back.

"Thank you. So can they start on Monday?"

"That should be fine, Januari. Thank you. We'll see you on Monday," said Felicity, smiling.

"Thank you. Goodbye," I smiled, and exited the building. I was quite pleased with how that went, at the time.

I headed back to my sisters, and we called for takeaway. I told June, July and Augusta that there'd be some nice people called Felicity and Ani looking after them while we were at school.

They seemed to be fine with that, just nodding and saying "Okay, Jannie," except Augusta, who was still getting the hang of talking. I knew they'd be all right, really. June and July were happy as long as they were together. Augusta just needed someone to look after her.

I went upstairs to tell Mum. I was determined to keep doing this, going to talk to her regularly just about normal everyday things, not to let her lose touch with reality.

"Mum, I've had to register June, July and Augusta for nursery. They can go there while we're all at school. Is that okay?"

"Yes. Thank you, Januari. Were you okay going by yourself?"

"Of course, Mum. It isn't far."

She nodded, "all right. How are you all doing at school?"

"Very well. How are you doing at work?"

She sighed, "not so well. I'll be all right, Jan," she hesitated, and then added, "you're all doing all right, aren't you?"

"Of course we are, but I'm afraid the same can't be said for you. Are you sure you're all right, Mum?"

"Oh, yes. Of course I am, dear," she said quickly. I sighed as I left. Mum never admitted to me or my sisters that she was unhappy. That was why there wasn't much we could do for her.

So that was how things went from then on. June, July and Augusta went to nursery during the day. We got along fine. My only worry was that my sisters wouldn't have as enriching a childhood as they could have with only an older sister looking after them. I also didn't want them to think that Mum didn't care about them, because I knew that she did, really, deep in her heart. I knew it.

I knew there'd be no holidays or anything like that. That was the kind of thing I'd never had, so I couldn't give them that, but don't doubt that I would have done if I could.

I sometimes took them on free days out to museums and the park. We couldn't go to the beach or the city or anything because we couldn't go anywhere out of walking distance. My heart ached to hear other children talking about trips to the coast, even within this county where I used to go, because I knew that my sisters couldn't have that.

Sometimes I would make us a picnic and we'd go to the park... it was fun. Sometimes we'd have nights in with takeaway and board games.

My daily routine on a normal school day as a ten-year-old went something like this: I'd get up at 5:30am every morning to feed Augusta, who was only a baby back then. I used to set an alarm on the clock, which was by my bed, but after a while I didn't need to do that any more; I'd get up instinctively. I'd sing Augusta my lullaby to get her to go back to sleep. Then I'd go back to sleep for a bit.

I would wake up again at 6:30am to make breakfast for my other sisters, and grab a piece of buttered toast and a glass of water. My sisters woke up at 7:15am, and I'd always have their breakfast – and their clothes, neatly folded – ready for them. I'd be in my clothes already, and I always got myself ready before they woke up.

I got June, July and Augusta dressed while my other sisters were dressing themselves. Then we'd set off. First, we all went to take the younger ones to nursery. Then we went to Oldgate Junior and Infant School. We went round to the infants' section to drop off April and May. Then, finally, we'd go to the juniors' section, and run in seconds before the bell went. It was inconvenient, but I couldn't think of a better way of doing things.

After school, I would go with Februari and March to the infants' section to pick up April and May. We'd then all go to nursery to pick up June, July and Augusta. When we got home, it was usually around half past four. I would put a film on for the younger ones, and watch the first ten minutes with them to get them settled, then I'd go and either call for takeaway or start cooking tea. We usually ate at around 5:30.

After tea, I would put Augusta to bed at 6:30. June and July would go to bed at 7:00. I put April and May to bed at 7:30, and Februari and March went at 8:00. I got everything ready for the following day, making sure everyone's clothes were folded by their bed, made sure my alarm was set... things like that, and I'd get to bed at about 8:30.

I put my heart and soul into looking after my sisters, gave it everything I could, tried so hard to make their lives the best they could be considering the way things were.

It meant that I couldn't go round to my friends' houses any more, no sleepovers or meeting up out of school, but there was nothing to be done about that. It was a sacrifice I had to make if I wanted my sisters to have everything I could give them. I could spend time with Genevieve, Jemima and Victoria at school only, which made it all the more precious.

Birthdays and Christmas were the most difficult because I always wanted to do something special for my sisters, as most children had for their birthday or at Christmas-time. I had to ask Mum for money to buy them presents.

Usually I would make a birthday cake myself, and sometimes I'd even have to make the present. Most of the time I'd be able to buy something. Usually I would end up wearing clothes that were too small to save the money, so I could use it for something else more important.

I rarely got birthday and Christmas presents myself, but I didn't mind, as long as my sisters had something.

Christmas was harder than birthdays, because I needed to find some way of getting presents for all my sisters. I could make Christmas cake myself, and my sisters all had stockings that I'd made for them. Usually I'd have to resort to buying an assortment of wool, and fabrics, and stuffing. I already had knitting and sewing needles, so all that was left was to make as many soft toys and the like as possible. I got better at making things as I got older, which was just as well because as I grew up, there were more sisters to look after.

So we got along fine, and I did everything I could. It was, perhaps, harder when I was younger because there was less that I was capable of doing.

As I grew older, people knew who I was – the people at the supermarket, Ani and Felicity... and everyone got used to the fact that I looked after my sisters.

"*Who's that kid going round the supermarket on her own?*" people would ask. "*Shouldn't someone be with her?*" and others who knew me would reply "*oh, that's just Januari. She looks after all her younger sisters – nice kid.*" It was nothing out of the ordinary any more and as people got used to me doing things for myself, I got used to it as well... hard work became a habit.

Chapter 5

Ito ay ang lahat sa ilalim ng kontrol

It's all under control – Filipino

The year I went to high school, things changed a lot. I had to think up a new way of doing things. For a start, another sister had been born the previous year – September Blaze Winters. I looked at her, and she looked at me, and I knew that it was down to me to look after this little girl. To raise her well and truly, right from the beginning. By now, Mum's mind had become so unbelievably, unrecognisably twisted that I wasn't sure she was even aware of the world around her. If I hadn't known better, I'd have said she was almost becoming a robot. Fortunately, I was well practised in looking after small children, so it wouldn't be a problem, but I wanted September to have the best childhood she could possibly have in these circumstances.

The catchment school was Oldgate High School. There were two high schools in our area, Oldgate and Newgate. As we lived in Oldgate, my friends and I were all going there.

My baby sister September loved people playing games with her, and would happily listen to March's stories all day as long as they had fairies and princesses and the odd mermaid in them. Though she had much rather turn them into a game.

One night, a few weeks after she was born, I stayed up all night making her a fairy doll. It was definitely a fairy, not a faerie. For me, there had always been a clear difference between the two.

Fairies were happy little winged people in little flower-like dresses dancing round toadstools with a constant smile on their faces. Faeries were mythical creatures, paranormal beings. No one knew what they looked like, but I was certain they weren't happy little winged people in pink dresses.

So I made a fairy doll for September and she loved it. We named it Rosie, and she still has it now. She loves playing games with it, she always has. I knew she'd like it.

Her first word was 'Princess' when the time came, but that wasn't for a while.

When I started high school, I had to think up a new routine. Things wouldn't have worked in the same way. I still got up early to feed September. I went with my sisters to Oldgate Junior and Infant school, then to drop off Augusta and September at nursery, then I had to run all the way to make it to school on time.

I usually rushed in just as they were taking the register. At times like this, I was thankful my name – Winters - was at the end of the register. This became normal, just Januari Winters, running in at the last minute as usual.

Augusta had grown to love nursery. There were lots of crafty things she could do there like finger-painting. She loved getting messy... it made me think of Jemima, whose parents said she was exactly the same when she was that age.

On the first day of high school, I dropped all my sisters off at the various places they had to be, and then ran all the way to Oldgate High School. I knew we were supposed to go to the hall, then our form tutors would take us to our form rooms. When I got to the hall, I saw that everyone else was already there.

My friends and I were all in the same form by sheer luck – 7MF, which stood for our form tutor's initials (Mrs Mayra Farley) – and I saw them sat together on the front row. I crept out to join them, and silently sat down next to them. They grinned at me understandingly.

Once we had got to our form rooms, and Mrs Farley had sorted everything out there, our first lesson was science. However, Mrs Farley wanted a word with me before we went. "Before I take you to your first lesson, I want to have a word with you. There, girl with the brown hair. What is your name?"

"Januari Winters, Miss."

"Well, Januari Winters, would you care to explain why you were late on your first day? It's hardly a good example to set to the people who are to be your fellow students, Head of Year, headmaster and form tutor for the next five years."

"I'm really sorry, Miss. It wasn't anything that could be helped. I had to get my sisters organised, and then I took Februari, March and April to the junior school, then I had to take May and the twins to the infants, and Augusta and the baby to nursery. Mornings are a bit of a rush, but I got here as fast as I could, I'm very sorry."

"Are you meaning to tell me that you have *eight sisters*, and it is your responsibility to look after them and take them where they need to go? A little girl of your age? Now do you really expect me to believe that?" Mrs Farley said patronisingly.

"Yes, Miss. I've done it since I was ten. I don't particularly want to talk about it, if that's okay. It's something I have just accepted, and those around me usually just accept it too. There's nothing to be done about it. I really am sorry for being late, but I promise the situation won't affect my schoolwork."

Mrs Farley seemed speechless. She stared at me, and I began to feel uncomfortable. Then, at last, she spoke: "I understand, Januari. If you ever need to talk to someone..."

"If I ever need to talk to someone, I can talk to my friends, or to Februari," I replied defiantly. She nodded, and led us to our first lesson.

In science, I was put next to Genevieve, as we'd been put in register order. I was very happy about this, because it meant that Genevieve wasn't next to someone who would mock her for her enthusiasm.

Our first topic was Space, and Genevieve was absolutely over the moon. Pun intended. She could study Astrophysics every day without getting bored, and in fact, that was her dream job. I was happy about this too; Space was absolutely fascinating. Mind-blowing, really, that something could be so incomprehensibly massive and we only knew about a tiny fragment of what was out there...

I got used to high school soon enough, and settled down into my new routine. When I was in Year 7, my sister Octoba Starlight Winters was born.

Octoba was very pretty. September seemed to get on very well with her new baby sister, and loved playing games with her. Octoba was perfectly happy to go along with it, and it was company for September.

In the next year, Februari started high school. On the first day, I told her that she could go ahead if she wanted to, so that she wasn't late. She said it was fine; she wanted to go with me. So we went together, after taking the rest of our sisters where they needed to go.

My friends and I met Febs at lunchtime, wanting to hear all about how her first morning had gone. She said that every teacher she'd met so far had inquired if she was Januari Winters' sister. She said she'd been very proud to hear what the teachers said about me. I felt slightly uncomfortable then...

I didn't really want the teachers to be judging Februari before they met her, based on what I was like. We were very different. We'd always been very different.

That year, two new girls moved into the neighbourhood. The two girls were in April's year. They naturally befriended each other, though everyone else wanted to be their friend as well. One of the girls was called Kay Davies, and the other, Kylie Terry.

Kay had long auburn hair and blue eyes. Kylie had cropped hair which was dyed gold, and green eyes. They both liked acting older than they were, and were constantly telling stories of boyfriends and make-up and fashion and pop music, and other pointless, boring rubbish.

April flared up at them once, telling them that they didn't know what they were getting themselves into, and that being the grown-up wasn't all it was cracked up to be. She told them that they were too young to have boyfriends, because the possibility of actually knowing their true love at that age was extremely unlikely, and even if they did, they shouldn't be into that sort of thing at this age anyway.

As one might imagine, Kay and Kylie didn't take too kindly to this. They told April that she was just jealous, trying to spoil their fun. They told her that she was nobody.

Oh, it still makes me furious to think of those stupid, selfish idiots saying such horrible things to my sister. Not just any sister either: April. Poor, nervous little April who had only been attempting to stand up for her beliefs.

When they found out more about our family, they teased her more. They told her that she didn't have a proper family, and that no one really cared about her and my poor sister believed every word they said.

I remember the day when she first came home upset. I was used to her shutting us out, but she seemed really despairing... I decided it was best that I at least knew what she was upset about.

I went into our room and saw her lying on her bed, sobbing. I'd got the rest of my sisters downstairs watching a film so she could have a bit of space.

"April?" I said gently, "are you going to talk to me?"

She ignored me, so I went and sat down next to her. "I can't keep the others out of this room forever, you know."

There was a moment's hesitation, and then she wrapped her arms around me. I held her tightly, and we sat in silence for a minute. "I love you, April. You know that, don't you?"

"Those girls – Kay and Kylie – they said that no one cares about me, and that I don't have a proper family."

"Well, that isn't true at all, is it? You have a family: you have me, and Februari, and March, May, June, July, Augusta, September and little Octoba, and you have Mum as well, and Father. We all love you. They're probably only saying that because they feel unloved. They probably have problems with their families, and they're just jealous of you, because you have a nice, big family that loves you very much."

"Really?"

"Really, and you're intelligent, and pretty, and a genuinely nice person, and so, so brave."

"I love you, Jannie. Thank you. For... everything."

"I love you too, April, and *don't you forget that.*"

She smiled, and went downstairs to join our sisters. I sat by myself for a minute longer, thinking.

I knew this must be affecting April dreadfully. Those harsh words would hurt anyone, and for them to be said to April... the consequences could be disastrous.

She just needed to be reminded that people loved her. I shouldn't let this get to me, I told myself. April would be fine. I was just worrying too much. If this problem blew over, I'd find some other reason to worry about my sisters.

I was just worried that I couldn't give them what a parent could give them. I wanted them to be happy, and to live normally. I'd given up on my life ever being normal that their lives might be. So I wasn't going to let two stupid little girls take away my sister's happiness. This was going to stop, right now.

Chapter 6

Cela devient plus facile tout le temps

It gets easier all the time – French

When I was in Year 9, November Scarlett Winters was born. She was a very *happy* baby, it reminded me a bit of May. May, however, had always been an attention-seeker, and November wasn't so much.

I made her a doll out of a pair of my old tights with a sewn-on smiley face and woollen plaits and a fabric dress, which she later named Maia. I did my best for her, because I wanted her to grow up and live happily. Her mother never paid much attention to her, and her father was ill, so I was the only parent figure in her life, but I wasn't her parent, only her sister. I couldn't give her what a parent could give her. I wished I could have done.

When I was in Year 11, my last sister was born. December Aurora Winters looked a lot like me.

When I left high school, I was already starting to feel left behind. I knew I wouldn't be able to go to college or take driving lessons. I knew that when I left high school, it would be time for me to settle down to a routine that I would be following for the next 20 years of my life.

My friends were all planning to study elsewhere in our home country of Larenia, so I was literally going to be left behind. They weren't leaving the country, but I wouldn't be able to see them. At least we could still write letters.

I was sad to leave Oldgate High School, because I had been happy there. I'd loved learning there; the teachers were friendly, and it really was a good school, but I hadn't been able to make the most of it.

I remember the day when my friends all left me to go and study in sunny Rosamontis. I knew they'd come back eventually, but I missed them.

It was during school time, so I went to the bus station with them to say goodbye. They were getting the bus to Veleda in Rosamontis. I suspected they'd make other friends while they were away, maybe even fall in love.

I told them I would miss them, and wished them luck. I told them they knew where I was if they needed me, and that they could contact me if they wanted.

Really, I was just wishing them all the best in their lives, which they had ahead of them. I hoped all their dreams would come true. I didn't doubt that they would. I knew my friends were all intelligent girls, and I was sure they'd live happily ever after.

After my friends were gone, I started wondering what I was going to do with my life. It seemed to be all planned out for me. I remembered the teachers saying not to get ahead of yourself, not to be older than you were.

I didn't seem to have a choice in the matter. I had to play the grown-up because there was no one else to do what was necessary.

I wasn't ever going to have a family of my own, only my sisters. Over time, I grew to hate the idea of falling in love. If I ever fell in love, it would only cause me pain, because no one would think about me in that way.

I would end up with my heart broken, and I'd just have to carry on as if nothing had happened. My very soul would be broken, its light extinguished. I would be dead inside, and no one wants that. So I grew to become afraid of falling in love.

The chance of that happening was very low, though. It wasn't as if I had a social life any more, so where would I meet someone like that? I contented myself with looking after my sisters, and giving them everything I could.

When I left high school, I took November and December out of nursery. They were so happy that they'd have their own sister looking after them instead of Ani. I was glad as well, because I could look after them myself. They could know me better, and it would help them to know that they could trust me.

I looked forward immensely to being able to look after my sisters properly. I would just be staying at home all day, with November and December for company. When my sisters came home from school, I would be there waiting for them. It would be really nice, and a lot easier.

The problem with Kay Davies and Kylie Terry only got worse. April stopped standing up for herself, and kept coming home crying. I tried convincing myself that I was doing everything I could, but I still felt as if it wasn't enough. I spoke to the school, I spoke to both the girls' parents, but nothing seemed to happen. I didn't stop doing all that I could to stop it.

I wanted April to be happy, just like I wanted the rest of my sisters to be happy. I'd sacrificed my happy ending for it. It seemed like a pretty fair exchange to me: my story wouldn't have a happy ending, but I could ensure that all my sisters could live happily ever after. The happy endings of eleven different stories in exchange for the happy ending of one story – my story. It was an exchange I was perfectly ready to make.

Februari told me she was sure I would get a happy ending, "Of course you'll get a happy ending, Januari. You work so hard to look after us, and to keep us happy; you've given up so much for us. One day, you'll meet someone who will appreciate how hardworking and brave and beautiful and intelligent and strong and determined and cheerful you are. He'll love you, and you'll love him. You'll realise that you do get a happy ending after all."

"I'm afraid that isn't the way things work, Febs," I said wearily, "firstly, I'm not any of those things you said. Secondly, we just have to accept that no one would be mad enough to love me. I'm just a plain, everyday girl with no social life. Thirdly, I spend all my time with you girls, and it can't be any other way."

"Jan... you know, hope has ways of showing itself at the most unlikely moments."

"You sound like you're quoting someone there, who told you that?"

"You did."

"Well..." I struggled to find a reply, "I didn't mean... I've known for a long time that I'm not going to get a happy ending. Just accept it, Febs."

"Well, aren't you saying that we're all going to get a happy ending?" she shot back at me.

"Yes, of course you are, so you should be happy about that. Don't worry about me."

"Well, what if our happy endings involve you living happily ever after?"

It took me a while to think of a response to that. Eventually, I replied, "well, you can't have a happy future if you're living in the past. You girls will all move on, and I'll get left behind. That's always what happens. You'll go off and live your lives, and before you know it... I'm just another blurry figure from your past."

"What you're doing for us... it leaves a lasting impression, Januari. You have to realise that. You're holding us all together. You're stepping into the place of the parent, and you mean more to us than any parent. Why have parents when you can have Jannie? That isn't something we're going to just forget."

"Thanks, Febs, but you will live happily ever after; you'll grow up and go to college and learn to drive, and one day you'll fall in love and get married and maybe even have a family of your own. You'll always know where I am and you can come round with your family whenever you want to visit your sister."

"Well, surely you're going to have to build a new life after December's grown up."

"Then I'll just have to have a quiet life on my own. I can get a job, and... live my life. It sounds quite appealing, really."

"Well, if that's what you really want, then that's your happy ending, isn't it?"

"I guess that's as happy as it gets."

"But it isn't what you really want, is it? I know you, Januari Snow Winters, and I know that you want to travel the world and find true love."

"Well, maybe I will travel the world one day. Then my dreams will be half-fulfilled."

"I'm sure you'll find true love as well. You *will* live happily ever after, Jan, I know it."

"I won't find true love, but I'm content with what I've got, Februari. Even now. There might not be romantic love, but there is love in my life. I love you, and all my sisters. You'll always be my sisters, no matter what. It's enough just to have friends and family."

"Well, just as long as you know you can have happiness," I hugged her tightly. I didn't know what I'd do without Februari. She kept me going. She gave me hope. I knew that, really, I was happy with the life I had, and I wouldn't exchange it for the world. All the hard work, the situation we were in... it made me who I was and my sisters were in it with me.

It made all the difference that I had my sisters. If I'd been an only child, there wouldn't have been any sisters to look after, so I wouldn't have been in this situation anyway. I would have been a totally different person. A world without my sisters, however, was unbearable to think about.

I loved them all – Februari with her constant faith in me, always there for me, my best friend. March with her creative spark, and all the wonderful stories she wrote. Little April and cheerful May. Girly July and tomboy June. Augusta with her artwork. September with her fantasy obsession. Little Octoba and November and baby December.

Just as much as they made me the person I was, I made them who they were. I was the one who helped March learn to read and write, who taught Augusta to paint and draw.

I suppose really my happy ending would be a comfortable life knowing that all 11 of my sisters were living happily ever after. I wouldn't get a happy ending, but they would, and that would be enough for me. I didn't care about my own happiness as long as my sisters were happy.

It would have been nice to find true love, but that wasn't going to happen. No one would love me, and I wouldn't allow myself to fall in love, so there was no possibility of any complications. It looked like my story was all planned out from here, and all I had to do was go and live it...

Part II

Shattered Expectations

One Year later

Chapter 7
Die Geschichte beginnt
The story begins – German

My life has never been like that of other girls my age. Everything about me seems to be unusual in some way or another. Even my name – Januari Snow Winters. Other kids used to tease me about it but soon gave up when they realised I couldn't care less what they say about me.

I *look* like any other 17-year-old girl - wavy oaken hair, shoulder length, and eyes swirling with several different shades of brown. Strange that such an unusual person would look so average... but I suppose you shouldn't judge a book by its cover.

Since I was ten, we haven't left town. There is no possibility of my taking driving lessons, what with my caring role for my sisters, so we have to walk everywhere. Mum gives me the money yearly, at the end of August, to get new clothes and school things if applicable.

Most of my sisters are at school. I left last year, and am now wondering what to do with my life, seeing that college is not a possibility, with 11 sisters to look after. It looks like my entire future is planned out for me already. Until December is grown-up, anyway, but I'll be 34 then, well into my life.

Don't get me wrong, I don't mind it. I love my sisters... I just wish I could raise them properly, and in a more enriching manner. To them, I am Jannie, or

Jan to the older ones, and I will always, always put them first.

As you may have deduced, I don't have much of a social life. My childhood friends – Jemima, Victoria and Genevieve – are all at college now. I don't have time to do anything other than look after my sisters but, as I said, I don't mind. Some people's lives are just like that. It could have been someone else, but, by chance, it was me. It's the way things are and there doesn't seem to be anything I can do about it at present.

Febs is now 16, and does her best to help me out with the others. She's still in high school, and she supervises March, April and May and walks to school with them.

Februari has long, straight, pale blonde hair, the colour of the inside of an almond, and brown eyes the same as mine. She's very pretty, and has lots of friends at school. She chooses not to meet up with them out of school, saying she'd rather be there in case I need her help for anything and I do, constantly. Dear, ever-faithful Februari... I don't know what I'd do without her.

March is 14 years old, and in Year 9. She often talks to Februari and me about different NLHE (National Larenian Higher Examinations) options; what they entail, and which ones we would recommend for her. You can tell March is dreading her NLHE years, but Februari is there for her at school and we're both there for her at home. Being there for my sisters when they need me is my priority. March has brown hair, like me, except that it is quite a bit darker and frizzier than mine, but her eyes are as blue as the sky in summer. March is the story-teller, always making up stories. She'll tell some of the more serious ones to Februari and me, and maybe April and May if she deems it appropriate, and the fairytale style ones to the younger children.

Shy April isn't as confident as the rest of us. She is 13, in Year 8, and she has problems with two of the other girls, Kay and Kylie, picking on her. I have been in to speak to the Oldgate staff about this issue and I am prepared to do it again if the situation worsens. I make sure that April can always talk to me if she needs to, and I can usually cheer her up. April has short, straight auburn hair, and pale blue eyes.

She's quite small, like most of our family are naturally small. Most of us are the small-but-fiery kind of small, but April is the small-and-very-timid kind and she finds things hard more frequently than the rest of us. Februari and March keep a wary eye on her at school as she walks round the corridors dejectedly, dragging her feet.

May is the opposite of April. She is in Year 7, 12 years old. April struggled with the transition, but May is loving feeling like one of the big kids. She is very boisterous, bouncy and bubbly. She runs everywhere with a skip in her step and is always bursting to tell me about her day at school. However, April doesn't usually feel the need to, but she knows when it's sensible to tell me she's upset. When she isn't telling me something important, I can tell.

May has blonde hair which is wavy and about the same length as mine and it bounces on her shoulders as she runs. Her eyes are bright and electric blue, and there is a light in them that never goes out.

June and July, now ten, are in Year 6 at school. They have long, straight blonde hair, and green-blue eyes, like the sea. They keep one another going and are constantly whispering to one another and giggling. They always wear friendship bracelets that the other one made. I have no idea what they talk about but I just leave them to it most of the time. If they need to talk to me, they will.

They are complete opposites, even though they're so close to each other. June normally ties her hair into a quick ponytail. She usually wears jeans and a t-shirt. She wouldn't be seen dead in any kind of skirt or dress. July is very girly, and likes to wear her hair down and wear skirts and dresses. They stick together though, despite their opposite personalities.

Augusta is eight, in Year 3. She has elbow-length wavy hair which is very dark brown, and green eyes. She loves drawing pictures, and the teachers at Oldgate Junior and Infant school often give her paper or a spare exercise book to draw in, understanding the situation at home. We have one set of colouring pencils, which is, of course, most frequently used by Augusta. Most days, she'll come home with a new picture she's drawn at school and present it to me proudly, explaining what everything is and saying it's for me. Every time, I will exclaim in surprise and give her a big hug and tell her it's a beautiful picture, and she'll beam back at me, her eyes alight with happiness. I can tell Augusta's going to be a great artist one day.

Six-year-old September has straight red hair down to her waist, and deep brown eyes much like mine. She is in Year 2, and is much enjoying being in the oldest class in the Infant School. She is always wanting to tell me about the latest game she and her friends have thought up to play at breaktime and lunchtime. September loves listening to the stories March tells, particularly the ones about princesses. She is always ready to play fairy princess games with her younger sisters the minute she gets home, and she says that she wants to be Rapensela when she grows up.

Octoba is five and spends most of her time at home playing little-girly games with September. Her favourite is the one where they are the princesses of the mer-fairies, which I hear about non-stop. Octoba's hair is long and wavy, and, like Augusta's, it is the precise colour of dark chocolate. She has blue eyes.

Sometimes September and Octoba come to me, asking me to play with them, which I will happily do. I am always prepared to look after my sisters. I pick up June, July, Augusta, September and Octoba from school, while Februari walks back with March, April and May.

November is three, and I always brush her red hair for her in the morning and put it in its usual bunches. Her eyes are green, the exact colour of fir trees. She loves playing games with dolls, which I am inclined to do with her all day while the others are at school.

Sometimes I'll put on a fairytale-style film for her to watch, then all I have to do is sit with her while she watches it. The two youngest are the most difficult to look after because they aren't at school yet so I have to keep them entertained all day with no money to take them out. Sometimes we'll go and feed the ducks in the park if we have some spare bread at the end of the week.

December is the baby, only a year old. She has brown hair and brown eyes, like me. She can crawl, but can't yet walk. She is nearly talking, and has said her first word – 'Jannie' – which she'll happily babble all day long. She'll raise a little fist and point at me, saying, "Jannie." I'll applaud her and say, "yes, December, I'm Jannie. Clever girl, December." Then she'll clap too, shrieking with laughter.

Keeping November and December entertained all day can be a difficult job sometimes, especially when they're tired which, thankfully, isn't that often, but I get along fine.

I still went to talk to Mum most evenings, and just chatted away about normal things, refusing to just let her fade away and lose touch with reality. I just talked about whatever there was to talk about. We visited Father every week as well. He was staying in a hospice and was showing no signs of getting better. When things were worse, he would spend time in the local hospital.

I took November and December out of nursery after I left school because I have nothing better to do during the day and I'd much rather look after them myself.

So that's all of us – me, Februari, March, April, May, June, July, Augusta, September, Octoba, November and December. It's quite strange, really, that there were 12 girls and not one boy.

I've never really given much thought to it before. I'd much rather have my own sisters, though, because most boys are extremely immature around the high school stage. I only knew a handful of boys that were mature when I was at high school. I'm just thankful for my sisters, glad that they are who they are and I wouldn't exchange them for the world.

Chapter 8
Η ιδέα
The idea - Greek

It was just another day when I came up with the idea that would change my life forever.

I was woken up by December crying at 5:00 am. My eyes were open the minute I heard her. I climbed out of bed with as much energy as I could muster and went over to December's cot.

She sleeps in the same room as me, along with Februari, March, April and May, and the room next to ours is shared by June, July, Augusta, September, Octoba and November.

The others sleep straight through the night, but, through training myself, I'm a very light sleeper. I have to be able to get up at a moment's notice in case one of my sisters has had a nightmare or if one of the younger ones has wet the bed.

I picked up December and held her close. "Shhhh, December," I whispered, "I'm here." I changed her nappy, then headed downstairs to heat up a bottle of milk for her. Once she was fed and changed, I sat down on the settee, rocking her gently. I began to sing her a lullaby, one I'd written myself which I always sang to my sisters to lull them to sleep.

"Be calm, unwind, as you lie in my arms this night,

Relax, keep still, as you let sleep carry you away-ay-ay

Let it go...all that stress and worry, and all that makes you nervous

Sleep in peace, for you are loved.

Sleep in peace, for you are loved,
Sleep, darling, sleep. Dream happy dreams..."

It worked; by the end of the song, December was fast asleep. I carried her back upstairs, taking care not to wake her, closed the door silently behind us, and then tucked December back into her cot. "Sleep well, my little December," I whispered. Then I kissed her forehead, and made my way back over to my bed. This had taken about 20 minutes, meaning I had approximately 70 minutes more sleep before I had to wake up again. So I slept for another hour and ten minutes and then my alarm went off for 6:30. I got ready then and went downstairs to make breakfast for my sisters, before grabbing a quick piece of bread and butter and a drink for myself. Mornings were usually a massive rush for my sisters, with 12 people to get ready and only one bathroom.

I always had their breakfast ready on the table for when they woke up at 7:15. I also made sure their clothes were ready and folded by their beds, though they usually were – my sisters won't ever cause me any extra hassle if they can help it.

Februari, March, April and May said goodbye to me, then picked up their bags and set off for school. June, July, Augusta, September and Octoba leave a little bit later, so I helped Octoba and November get dressed while the others dressed themselves. I then dressed December, and strapped her into her pram.

When I had them all ready, we set off for school. I dropped off the juniors first, as their lessons run to a more precise timetable, commencing five minutes before the infants' area of the school. Mrs Banks, the head of the juniors, smiled at me. I smiled back, before saying goodbye to June, July and Augusta. "Have you got everything, girls? Yes? All right then, have a good day. Goodbye June, goodbye July, goodbye Augusta. I love you."

They went skipping off in the direction of their classroom, and I smiled and waved after them. Mrs Banks came down to greet me, "hi, Januari, how are you doing?"

"Fine, thank you, Mrs Banks. How are you?"

"Very well, thanks, Januari. How are the others?"

"They're doing great. May is loving high school. I don't really have time to talk right now, I'm sorry."

"You say that every time I try to make friendly conversation."

"Oh, I'm so sorry about that. It's not that I don't want to talk, I just..."

"It's okay. I understand. You always seem to be in a hurry. Make sure you don't work yourself *too* hard, Januari. It seems only yesterday you were one of the younger ones yourself. You were very intelligent. We might even have mistaken you for a teacher and now... look at you. *17 years old.* My, how time flies." And then it hit me.

"*Of course,*" I breathed, "why didn't I think of that before?"

"I'm sorry, what? I don't think I understand you, Januari."

"I've just had an idea..."

"Ah, of course. A girl like you must be full of good ideas. I'll let you get on."

"Yes... it was nice talking to you."

"Goodbye, Januari. Remember what I said."

“I most definitely will. Thank you.”

I began ushering September and Octoba towards the infants’ area. Mr Mills is the head of the infants. He’s been at the school the longest – Mrs Banks was new when I started in Year 3. Mr Mills has known me since I was four. He smiled now as I approached him. September and Octoba scurried off inside.

“Bye, girls,” I called after them, “have a good day.” I shook my head, smiling. September had come up with a new game the night before and couldn’t wait to share it with her friends. Octoba followed wherever September went.

I stood there for a moment, with November holding my hand and December in her pram in front of me.

“Good morning, Januari,” said Mr Mills.

“Good morning, Mr Mills,” I replied, “how are you?”

“I’m perfectly well, thank you. I’m guessing you don’t have time to talk...?”

“You guess right,” I said, “I’m sorry, I don’t have the time to do anything, really.”

“No, I understand. Well, perhaps understand wouldn’t be the right word, I certainly don’t know what it’s like to raise 11 younger siblings, but I sympathise.”

“I don’t need sympathy. It’s my everyday life, and I’m fine with that.”

“Are you sure you aren’t working yourself too hard?”

“Of course not,” I said airily, “I’ve done it since I was ten.”

He smiled, "I'll see you later then, Januari. Have a good day - and take care of yourself."

"Of course. Same to you. Goodbye, Mr Mills," I set off home with November and December, anxious to plan out my idea, seeing if it could actually work...

When we arrived back home, I put on a cartoon for November and December. November loves watching films, and it keeps December quiet. I don't put films on too often, so it's a treat for the girls when I do, but sometimes I need to think, and it helps.

Mrs Banks had said *you were very intelligent. We might even have mistaken you for a teacher and now look at you... 17 years old.* So, if I looked a bit older, and played to my strengths... could I get away with being a teacher? I'd have to go somewhere no one would recognise me... Newgate High School. It would have to be. I could put November and December back in nursery... I didn't like it, but there was no other way around that.

I'd have to tell quite a few lies about experience, qualifications... obviously my age... and I knew that some of the teachers from Oldgate knew some of the Newgate teachers, so I'd have to go by a different name.

I didn't like the idea really, but it would get us some extra money. I could make life marginally better for my sisters. It would mean a lot of hard work, but I was prepared to work hard. It was what I did. I would talk to Februari about it later, and look to see if there were any vacancies at Newgate High School...

Later that evening, I proposed my idea to Februari.

"It was just a thought... but do you think this could actually work? We'd have more money... and you girls could have a proper childhood."

"We *have* had a proper childhood, Jan. You made sure of that. If it has been a bit...well... frugal, that is not your fault. I know you blame yourself that we've had it a bit harder than other kids, but... where would we be without you? If you hadn't been prepared to step up and do what you have done for us, we'd probably be scattered across the country in separate foster homes. Don't be so hard on yourself, Jan. We love you."

"I did what any decent person would do, but that's beside the point. What do you think about my idea?"

"I don't know, Januari... it would be a lot of extra work to take on... are you sure you can take on the challenge?"

"Febs, my whole life is taking on challenges. I could do it, fine, but I might have to come home slightly later... what about picking the girls up from school? November and December would have to go back in nursery."

"I know you could do it. I have complete faith in you. How about if I went home after school, dropped off March, April and May, and left them for five minutes or so while I went to pick up the younger ones..."

"If you were prepared to do that, Febs, this could actually work! You're a star, thank you. Then I could pick up November and December from nursery after I'd finished work... yes!"

"Don't get excited, Jan. Let's look and see if there are any staff vacancies first."

So I went to the computer, and found the Newgate High School website. I looked at the vacancies page, and the following notice glared out at me from the screen.

Language teacher wanted urgently!

Newgate High school is in urgent need of an addition to our language staff. Lessons are currently being taken by supply teachers. Candidates would have to speak Citanian, Mysterian and Wisilian. Candidates with experience would be preferable, but not essential. We would welcome applicants who are newly qualified. Interested candidates should come directly to the Language Office at Newgate High School on a Saturday or Sunday afternoon before 20th February.

Thank you.

Mr B. Marsden, Head of Languages

Brian Marsden

"Februari..." I whispered.

"Wow," she said, "that's perfect. You know how good you are at languages... okay, I admit it, that job was made for you."

"I'd better start thinking up lies because I'll have to tell an awful lot of them in order to pull this off."

"Yep... but you're really going to do this? For us?"

I grinned: "Let's do this thing."

The next day, while the girls were at school, I took November and December to nursery to see about getting them a place. Ani was now about 25 and running the nursery since Felicity had retired. Ani had straight black hair, and her eyes were a kind of lilac shade. She was the kind of person everyone liked. Her face split into a wide smile when she saw me.

"Hi, Januari," she greeted me, "I haven't seen you in a while."

I smiled back at her. "Hi, Ani," I said, "I've been thinking of getting a job recently, and I'm going to apply on Saturday. If I get the job, it'll be full time, so I'll need somewhere for November and December to stay during the day, until around half four-ish. You're the first place I come for childcare, so I was wondering if there were any places going spare."

"Wow, you do get to the point quickly, don't you?" she replied, still smiling, "now, as it happens, there are places going spare. I'd definitely be able to take them. Weekdays, right?"

"Yep."

"Well, I'll reserve two places for you, and give me a bell after you find out if you've got it or not. Knowing you, Januari Winters, I'm sure you will, but good luck, anyway."

"Thanks, Ani, that'd be great."

"Happy to help. I'm guessing you don't want to linger. I could make you a cup of tea or something...?"

"It's a very tempting offer, but you're right. I need to get back home, really. Thanks a lot, Ani."

"You're welcome, Januari. I'll probably see you soon, then."

"Bye, Ani."

Smiling to myself, I left the Sparkling Waters Nursery. November jumped up at me, "Jannie, are we going to nursery?"

"You might be, Nova. I'm sorry about that."

"It's ok. I like Ani. We'll miss you, though."

"I'll miss you too, November." December was fast asleep in her pram. I took extra caution that she should stay that way as we headed homewards. I planned to be extra nice to my sisters in the time I had with them before I went to work.

Chapter 9
מתוקה הצלחה
Sweet Success - Hebrew

The days passed as usual until Saturday came. I planned to go to Newgate in the afternoon, leaving myself plenty of time to prepare. In the late morning, I prepared myself. I found an old school shirt and some school trousers, which thankfully still fitted.

Then I brushed my hair. I had decided on the name 'Janet Woods' to go by. It wasn't so different to my real name, and I'd get along fine. I reckoned I could get away with 21 at the oldest, so that was my plan. I hurried downstairs to make sandwiches for lunch, and feed December. After all this was done, I was ready to go. I neatened up my hair, and went to talk to Februari.

"Okay, Febs, I'm going. How do I look?"

"You look very... formal and older."

"Good. That's the point. You're sure you'll be all right?"

"Of course I will. It's only for an hour or so. Don't worry about it."

"Thanks, Februari. I'll see you soon."

"Bye, Jan. Good luck."

"Bye, Febs."

I said goodbye to all my other sisters as well, then set off. Newgate wasn't far away, about one or two miles walk. When I arrived, I started looking for the language office. I wandered round the corridors, sure that I'd find it eventually.

I eventually realised I'd have to ask someone for directions. I saw a man walking past, and spoke to him.

"Excuse me, sir?"

He looked up. He had straight, short, dark brown hair and grey eyes. He looked quite young, only a few years older than me. He wasn't smiling, but nor was he frowning; his expression was neutral. He seemed to be deep in thought. I wondered vaguely whether it might have been a mistake asking him.

"Yes?" he replied.

I took a deep breath.

"My name is Janet Woods. I'm here about the vacancy in the Language Department, and I was wondering if you might be able to point me in the direction of the Language Office."

"Yes... of course. I'll show you the way." We walked in silence, me slightly behind him, letting him lead the way. After a while, he spoke again: "I should probably introduce myself. My name is Mr Derby, I'm a Larenian teacher here... I'm sorry, I'm not really used to talking to people, except when I'm teaching."

"That's all right. I don't talk much either. Moments of silence are scarce in my life... I value them." We passed the rest of the way in silence, then stopped outside the room.

"Well... this is the Language Office. Good luck, Janet."

"Thank you."

"Should I come and find you afterwards, to show you the way back?"

This offer surprised me, as I was still a stranger to him and he didn't seem a very sociable person. Knowing me, I would probably have something else on my mind on the way back and would wander off in the opposite direction, so I thought it best to take him up on this offer.

"That would be very helpful, thank you, Mr Derby."

He nodded, "I'll see you soon, then."

"Yes... thank you again."

I turned to face the door of the language office. I knocked.

"Come in," called a voice. I took a deep breath, and entered.

I left about an hour later feeling very lightheaded, scarcely able to believe it. Somehow, amazingly, *I'd got the job.* Mr Derby was lingering outside, waiting. "Well, how did it go?" he inquired as we started walking.

"I got the job."

"I'm glad to hear it. Congratulations."

"Thank you." We walked the rest of the way, as we had the way there, in silence. When we arrived at the exit, I thanked him again.

"You're welcome. I'll see you on Monday."

"See you on Monday." I felt very peculiar as I left. It was a good feeling. I couldn't quite believe I'd actually got the job. The head of languages - Brian Marsden- had been very friendly, and given me all the information I needed to start work. Thankfully, he hadn't asked for proof of my achievements at college and university. I was sad to have had to tell so many lies to such nice people, but I was contented to think that at least I had a valid reason for doing so.

It had been almost too easy to get the job – of course, no proof of former achievements... just like that. It seemed very unrealistic really, I couldn't quite believe I'd actually got away with it. I supposed it had only been because Newgate needed a new language teacher so urgently, and Brian had skipped a few vital processes in order to find one immediately.

My sisters were extremely pleased to hear of my success. I suppose a normal family would have gone out for a meal to celebrate, but we aren't a normal family, so for tea I cooked us chicken and chips with a few vegetables. Februari offered to cook tea for me, but I insisted upon doing it myself – she's doing enough that I should be doing at the moment.

That evening, I called Ani to inform her of my success.

"Hey, Ani, I got the job."

"Wow, congratulations! I knew you'd do it. So we're on for Monday?"

"Yeah... are you sure you don't mind?"

"Of course not. It is literally my job, after all. So did you do anything special to celebrate?"

"No... you forget who you're talking to."

"Oh! I'm sorry, I didn't mean..."

"I know. Don't worry about it. Bye for now, Ani. I'll see you on Monday morning."

"See ya!" I hung up, smiling. My working life was ready to go.

Chapter 10
Nýja vini
A new friend – Icelandic

That Monday, I went about my usual morning routine. I wore a plain top and trousers. I took June, July, Augusta, September and Octoba to Oldgate Junior and Infant School while Februari took March, April and May to the high school. After delivering November and December to nursery, I got to Newgate High School as fast as I could.

"Good morning, Janet," Brian greeted me, "are you ready for your first day at work?"

"Yes. I'm ready."

"That's what I like to hear. I wish some of the other teachers had your attitude. I have your timetable here," he held it out and I took it. It was a Monday of the first week, and the timetable ran over a two-week period. "You have a Year 9 Mysterian class first."

"March's age," I muttered to myself. Then I said to Brian, "okay, and that classroom is...?"

"Just round the corner. You'll find it."

"All right... well, I'd better go and prepare for my first lesson, then!"

"Yes... Good luck, Miss Woods."

"Thank you, Brian."

I'll need it, I thought to myself as I went into the classroom which my timetable told me I needed to go into, and made sure the Year 9 Mysterian Class's exercise books were ready. I looked at the lesson plans made by the supply teachers, and saw that the current topic was 'Csxsxuibwa osasssa' – past holidays.

A few minutes later, my first class entered the room. I smiled in what I hoped was a confident, authoritative way, and they all sat down in what were clearly their allocated seats and looked at me expectantly. I took a deep breath, and began.

"Giks, ks xksr. Nu kksni Awbieurs Woods. Ait cywares oeidwaies sw Ntarweusb oie warw sbi. Now, who can translate that?"

A girl at the back of the classroom raised her hand.

"Au? ¿Xini rw kksnss, Awbieurs?"

"Nu kksni Mia Casey, and you said 'Hello, class. My name is Miss Woods. I am your Mysterian teacher for this year'."

"Yes, that's right, Mia. That's exactly what I said. Well done. Now, I'm going to do the register. I want you to answer me 'Au, Awbieurs.' Then I'm going to explain how things are going to work in my lessons."

So I did the register, then tried talking to them in a way that I would have wanted a teacher to talk to me at Oldgate.

"So, I'm not going to be too strict with you, I'm going to try to be reasonable. This is my first job as a teacher, so if I do something wrong, just don't be scared of telling me, okay? I don't bite. Don't be afraid to talk to me, but that doesn't mean I'll let you get away with everything, I am still your teacher. So follow normal class rules, and... I'll do my best to be a good teacher. If your behaviour's good, I might get rid of the seating plan. Does that sound okay to you?"

They nodded, so I continued with an "all right, then let's get started..." and then I taught my first lesson. Afterwards, one of the students – Mia – came to talk to me.

"Thank you, Miss Woods. I thought that was a really good lesson."

"Was it all right for you?"

"Yes. You're a very good teacher."

"I'm glad you think so."

"I think the students will be able to relate to you well. You were fantastic. I really enjoyed that lesson."

"Thank you for saying so, Mia. It helps me to feel better about... lots of things. You were a very good student as well. You're very intelligent."

"Thank you, Miss. Ssuia."

"Gsars kywfi. I'll see you next lesson, Mia. Now, I'm supposed to be in Wi4 next lesson... do you know where that is?"

"Yes. It's just near...I'll show you the way."

"Thanks, Mia, that's really helpful."

My next lesson was a Year 8 Wisilian class. That went quite as well as the first one, I thought. The students at Newgate all seemed really nice. With a few exceptions, of course. I was very pleased with how my first morning went. During breaktime, I sat in the language office and read my book.

I was re-reading a book on the history of philosophy in Larenia. I loved that book because it was so intriguing. It had taught me so much. Before I read that, I didn't know much at all about Suxtaro and Piero. I'd studied Atudriko in school, of course, but after reading that book, I didn't like him as much. Suxtaro and Piero were wiser men by far. Reading it gave me a different view on life.

I was sitting alone in the room, so it surprised me when I heard someone saying, "hello, Janet." I started, and quickly slid my bookmark in and looked up to see who'd spoken. It was Mr Derby.

"Hello, Mr Derby. I was just..."

"Reading. Of course... it does put the mind at rest, doesn't it?"

He glanced at my book, "ah, a very good choice. Have you read it before?"

"Yes, I have. It's a very good book. Absolutely fascinating."

"I agree completely. It really does whisk you away to another world, it's a great way of escaping. So how did your first morning go?"

"Better than I expected. One of the students actually came to me afterwards and said she enjoyed the lesson."

"Excellent. Students never talk to me. They all seem to hate me."

"I bet that isn't true."

"Trust me, they do. I try my best... at least they learn something... well, I'll leave you to read your book."

"Okay. It was nice talking to you. I'll see you later, Mr Derby."

"Goodbye, Janet."

He nodded, and I smiled, and then he left the room and I read my book for the remainder of the 15-minute breaktime.

My next class was Year 10 Citanian. They were actually only two years younger than me, and I didn't have a sister that age at that time, so I was more nervous about teaching this class, but it went fine. One of the boys came to find me afterwards.

"Miss... how old are you?"

"Why are you asking, Ray?"

"Well... it's just..."

"Come on, tell me. I don't bite."

"Well, please don't think I'm being cheeky, but you only look about 17."

I shuddered at the accuracy of his guess. "I'm 21."

"Sorry..."

"It's okay. You were just curious. Curiosity is not a bad thing. Asking questions is good, if you honestly just want to know the answer."

"Okay. See you, miss."

"Bye, Ray."

After that was the lunch break, so I had my lunch, and then went for a wander around the corridors to try to find out where all the classrooms were, so I'd know my way around my work better.

"Janet!" Brian Marsden hurried over to me, "hi, I've been meaning to ask you how your first morning went."

"I think I did all right. It was good. I was just trying to learn where all the classrooms are."

"You don't have to know them all by heart, don't worry. We don't expect that from you quite yet."

"Well, I do. In my opinion, it's my responsibility as a teacher to know where the classrooms are."

"Well then, you're one step ahead of us. Thank you, Janet."

"You're welcome."

I saw Mr Derby standing nearby, apparently deep in thought, and started walking towards him, meaning to say hello.

"I wouldn't do that if I were you, Janet," said Brian quickly. I stopped walking, and turned to face him.

"Why not?"

"That's Mr Derby. He's... a bit of a loner. None of us have been able to befriend him. I don't even think he *has* any friends. He never smiles... sometimes I wonder whether he even has a heart in there. I would stay away from him if I were you."

"I've already met him. He seems nice to me, and he may not have any friends but that doesn't mean he likes being alone. I form my own opinions, and from what I know of him so far, I think he's a nice person."

"Well, talk to him if you want, I'm not going to stop you. Maybe you can work a miracle. I would strongly advise against it, but if you think he's going to treat you differently to anyone else, then please proceed."

I ignored the sarcasm in his voice.

"Thanks, I will," I replied coolly, and walked over to where Mr Derby was standing, "hello, Mr Derby," I greeted him.

"Hello, Janet," he said in an amused-sounding voice, "I take it you are completely ignoring the advice Brian Marsden just gave you."

"You heard all of that?"

"I'm not deaf, you know."

"Most people would be upset to hear other people talking about them in that way; are you all right?"

He shrugged, "I'm used to it. Most of what he said was right, anyway. I haven't smiled in a long time and I don't have any friends. However, I do have a heart. I'm just... people aren't usually nice to me. For me, the world is a cold, dark and lonely place. Other people just tease, and mock, and cause pain, and pretend to be your friend, then stab you in the back. I've never really met anyone who's been sincerely nice to me before. You'd be the first."

I looked at him, not sure what to make of it. I answered him, "like I said, I form my own opinions, and I trust my instincts, and my instincts are telling me that you are a nice person. Nicer than Brian."

"He thinks he knows me, but he doesn't. He's only trying to help, though I'm not sure how, and... the reason I don't have any friends... well, no one would want to be friends with me, would they? Not that I blame them." His voice sounded bitter.

"I would," I said quietly.

"I'm sorry, what?"

"I'd want to be your friend."

"Really? But... why?"

"You're a good man, Mr Derby. Besides, I trust my instincts."

That was actually a lie. At that moment, my instincts were screaming that this was a very bad idea. If I had friends here... well, I didn't want anyone getting close enough to me to discover my secret. *It's all right just to have friends.* I told myself... *and Mr Derby... you know you want to be his friend.* There was a huge war going on inside my head, but eventually the 'Just relax, you're allowed to have friends; don't be so strict with yourself' side got the better of me.

"So, friends then?" he asked, holding out a hand. I shook it.

"Friends," I smiled. He still wasn't smiling, but he had a strange expression on his face.

"I've never had a real friend before."

"...Well, now you have."

"I'm glad it's you." Then the bell rang, meaning we had to go to prepare for our next lessons.

"I'll see you later, Mr Derby."

"Oh, and Janet..."

"...Yes?"

"Thank you. For what you said to Brian. For seeing the best in me."

"You're welcome," I smiled, and we headed off in separate directions to teach our next lessons.

When I got home, the rest of the afternoon went normally. I picked up November and December from nursery on the way back.

Februari wanted to hear all about my day, of course. I went about my usual routine for the rest of the evening: making tea, making sure all my sisters went to bed at the right times. While I cooked, I looked properly at my two-week timetable. It went something like this:

Monday 1	Reg.	9My3 My1	7Wi2 Wi4	10Ci1 Ci6	10Wi3 Wi2	8Ci6 Ci5
Tuesday 1	Reg.	7My4 My3	10Wi3 Wi2	11Wi2 Wi3	Free Period	9Wi2 Wi1
Wednesday 1	Reg.	9Wi2 Wi1	11Ci3 Ci1	10Ci1 Ci6	11Wi2 Wi3	8Ci3 Ci3
Thursday 1	Reg.	8My5 My2	9My3 My1	10Wi3 Wi2	11Ci3 Ci1	7My4 My3
Friday 1	Reg.	7Ci9 Ci5	Free Period	7Wi2 Wi4	8Ci6 Ci5	11Wi2 Wi3
Monday 2	Reg.	10Ci1 Ci6	9Wi2 Wi1	11Ci3 Ci1	8Ci3 Ci3	7Ci9 Ci5
Tuesday 2	Reg.	8Ci3 Ci3	11Wi2 Wi3	9Wi2 Wi1	7Ci9 Ci5	9My3 My1
Wednesday 2	Reg.	10Wi3 Wi2	7Wi2 Wi4	11Wi2 Wi3	10Ci1 Ci6	Free Period
Thursday 2	Reg.	11Ci3 Ci1	Free Period	7My4 My3	10Ci1 Ci6	8My5 My2
Friday 2	Reg.	8Ci6 Ci5	8My5 My2	11Ci3 Ci1	9My3 My1	10Wi3 Wi2

Later that evening, after all my sisters had gone to bed, I wrote a letter that I never intended to send. I addressed it to Father. It was like a diary entry, but these were things I wished I could tell Father, but was surrounded by Mum and my sisters. I would have told him if I could talk to him alone. I never intended to send the letter, or for anyone to read it, but it helped just to write it. I wrote:

Dear Father,

Since I was ten, I've been looking after my sisters because Mum just finds it too hard without you. I don't blame her, I know how much you mean to her. I got a job as a teacher. I lied about my name and age. I said my name was Janet Woods, and that I was 21 years old. I needed the job. I just wanted to be able to afford more for my sisters. You would be so proud of them all now.

I am now a language teacher at Newgate High School, and I'm hoping I'll be able to give my sisters a better life. Today was my first day at work. I did better than I expected I'd do.

I have a new friend there – Mr Derby, a Larenian teacher. I really wasn't sure if I did the right thing, I hope I did. The thing is, I don't want anyone finding out the truth about who I really am, because then I'd just lose my job. Who'd hire a 17-year-old?

I told myself it's all right to relax and to have friends. That I don't need to be so strict with myself. I do need to be careful, though. It's just that he's so nice to me, and he likes the same things I do... I just really want to be his friend. I suppose it will all be all right, as long as no one finds out my secret. I really, really hope I did the right thing.

Love, Januari

Chapter 11

La panchina nel parco

The bench in the park - Italian

The next day was easier. I went to work, and knew what to expect. I was ready.

I did just as well teaching lessons as I did the previous day. I really felt like this was a routine I'd like getting used to. It wouldn't be hard at all.

The previous night, Februari had been going on about some guy she apparently had a crush on. When I was in high school, I hadn't really done the whole boyfriend-girlfriend thing. I didn't see the point in it. If you were lucky enough to find real, true love, it certainly wasn't going to be at that age. If my sisters wanted to do that kind of thing just to keep things interesting, I wasn't going to stop them, though. It was their choice, really.

Either way, she was telling me about this Alfie Barker or whatever his name was. She said he was very good looking, and had a good sense of humour. Good looks didn't matter to me at all. Februari and I were very different in all aspects. I listened to her going on about him all evening, sounding very popular-teenage-girly. Which would make sense, seeing as she is exactly that.

I had a pile of books to mark by this point, so I did that at breaktime, and got lots of them done. I finished doing this at lunchtime, then read my book for a bit. Brian and a few other members of the language staff whose names I didn't know sat talking.

I didn't mind. I didn't really feel like talking to them, especially not Brian. I hadn't thought he was a judgemental person, but he seemed to be. I preferred to keep to myself.

A short while later, there was a knock on the door.

"Come in," called Brian.

Mr Derby came in, looking hesitant. I knew how he must be feeling – Brian only seemed to talk about him behind his back, and the others seemed perfectly fine with this. Brian seemed surprised when he saw who was coming through the door, seeming to regret welcoming him in.

"Mr Derby... hello."

"Good day, Brian," he looked at me, "hello, Janet."

"Hello, Mr Derby," I smiled at him, "how are you?"

"The same as ever. I was wondering if you wanted to go for a walk with me. You don't have to if you don't want to."

"No, that would be nice."

Trying to ignore the incredulous expression on Brian's face, I got up and put my book away. Then I went over to Mr Derby, and we left the room.

"What is Brian's problem?" I asked as we headed down the corridor.

"He thinks he knows me," replied Mr Derby, "he thinks I'm... some kind of anti-social, heartless... thing. He also probably thinks I'm depressed and he thinks I'm your stereotypical strict teacher."

"Wow... why don't you prove him wrong?"

"Well... I'm not really that bothered what he thinks about me. His opinion isn't important, really."

"You sound exactly like me. I don't care what other people think as long as I'm doing the right thing for me."

"Yes, I'm exactly the same. Besides, it's a good way of telling what new teachers are going to be like. If they completely ignore me and treat me like a display on the wall, I'll know that they judge people before they've met them. That's been all of them so far except you, really."

We headed out of the school grounds, and into the park next to it. We wandered along until we found a bench, and then we sat down.

"My sister's been telling me about some guy she has a crush on. She's 16, in Year 11, but at Oldgate. I'm not exactly sure how to react."

"Well, don't you understand that? I thought all people were into boyfriends and girlfriends as high school students"

"No, I don't. I think the whole thing is kind of pointless, actually. I mean, what is the likelihood of meeting your one true love at that age? No, I don't do that whole thing. It's something to be avoided, in my opinion. As for true love... that isn't going to happen to me, either. There's a... situation...at home, which means that I have no social life, and I'm just an average girl, so...not for me."

"Me neither. The no social life thing is kind of my choice, but... I'm just that teacher from Newgate who never smiles. I used to dream about true love, but I suppose I got used to the world being dark, and... I gave up on that dream a long time ago. So what are you going to say to your sister?"

"I have no idea. I mean, she expects me to relate, and I... don't. Her supposed crush is called Alfie Barker, and-"

"*What?!* Barker? Are you sure? Alfie Barker?"

"Yes," I said, slightly alarmed, "his brother and him moved into the area last year... why?"

"I knew his brother, as a child..." he shuddered, "he was the worst person I ever met. He used to call me names, and... all he cared about was himself. All he cared about in girls was how pretty they were."

My heart sank. If Alfie Barker was anything like the brother Mr Derby spoke of, Februari was making a big mistake. I decided to give him a chance. Siblings were often very different. Hopefully Alfie Barker would be a nice person.

"I hope for your sister's sake that Alfie Barker is the complete opposite of his brother," said Mr Derby.

I noticed that he looked pale, and his face was unreadable.

"Are you all right, Mr Derby?"

"Yes, I'm fine. It's just... Jake Barker is back in the neighbourhood. It's only a matter of time before he finds me, and he's always done everything he can to make my life miserable. He used to take away everything that was precious to me. Thank goodness there isn't really anything to take. There's nothing that's particularly precious to me now."

I suddenly became aware of the time. I glanced at my watch. It was 1:15.

"Well, we'd better be getting back to work," I said, "it was really nice talking to you, Mr Derby... and if you want to talk to someone...well... you know where I am."

"Thank you, Janet."

We went back to school, and then headed off in our separate directions.

When I got back from work that evening, Februari hurried over to me.

"Hey, um... Jan?" she said quietly, "you might want to go up and talk to April. She's upset again, and she won't talk to anyone. I've tried, but she never listens to me."

"Oh, not again. Poor April. I really do worry about her sometimes."

"Don't worry, Januari. It's nothing you can do anything about."

"Yes, I can, and I will. I'm going to talk to her, and then I'm going to Oldgate High School to talk to the teachers. April *will* be happy. This is going to stop *right now.*"

Chapter 12
私の妹台無しにしないでください
Do not mess with my sister - Japanese

I went upstairs to find April crying in our room. In case I haven't mentioned before there are three bedrooms in the house. The first is Mum and Father's room. The second is my room, which I share with Februari, March, April, May and December. The third is the bedroom of June, July, Augusta, September, Octoba and November. It was pretty cramped, as one might imagine, and we spent most of our time in the lounge or somewhere else.

So I went over to April, and sat down next to her on her bed.

"All right, what have they done now?" I asked, trying to use as calm and sympathetic a voice as possible. She sniffed, and put her arms around me.

"They said... that I don't have any friends, and that I never will. That I'm a failure. That all I do is moan and cry all the time," she said mournfully.

"Oh, for goodness sake! The only reason you're sad so often is because they're ruining your life! You mustn't let them get to you so, April. You've just got to prove them wrong."

"But what if they're right?"

"They aren't! You can't think like that. You just have to show them that you don't care what they say. I know you do, but if they don't think you do, they won't see the point in picking on you any more. Their stupid opinions shouldn't matter to you, anyway. Who are they to hurt you like this?"

"Really, I *don't* have any friends."

"Well, why don't you ask May if you can hang out with her and her friends?"

"May doesn't want her big sister hanging around with her friends. They're all really girly as well... I wouldn't fit in."

"Perhaps you're right... well, how about March then?"

I knew spending time with March would do April a lot of good. March was optimistic, but not overly cheerful. She could introduce April to some good books, and then April would have friends in fiction. I knew March and her friends wouldn't mind having April with them, either.

April considered, "all right, then. Are you sure March won't mind?"

"Positive. And you know what they say – there's always room for a small one."

"Okay. Thanks, Jannie."

"You're welcome."

I decided I'd talk to March about that when I got back from Oldgate High. Right now, this was my priority.

I said goodbye to Febs, warning her not to tell April where I was going, then headed out of the door and along the road in the direction of Oldgate High School.

When I got there, I sought out the person who had the most influence in the situation: April's Head of Year. Mr Decker was a history teacher, and had started working at Oldgate when I was in Year 8. He was a tall man in his fifties, with greying hair and deep brown eyes.

I found his classroom, and knocked. "Come in," called a voice. I entered, thinking about what to say. I didn't want to sound too cross, because it wasn't the school's fault. I knew Oldgate was an excellent school, but I also needed them to know it was a matter of urgency. Mr Decker smiled when he saw me.

"Good evening, Januari. What can I do for you?"

"Well, the problem with April seems to be continuing. She's coming home upset more frequently than ever, and... I'm worried about her. It's those same two girls, Kay and Kylie. I was wondering if there was anything you could do?"

"Well, you do get to the point quickly, don't you?"

"You're not the first person to say that to me."

He laughed, "why does that not surprise me? Anyway, I'll certainly speak to both of their parents regarding the issue. Have you talked to April about this?"

"Yes, I have. One of the problems is that she actually believes what they say about her."

"Poor April. I may have a solution to part of the problem."

"Yes?"

"There are two new students starting next week. Raul and Mary Acevedo. I could put them in April's form. They are twins, and have moved here from Citania. You know, of course, about the civil war going on in Citania at the moment."

"I can see why they wanted to move, but Citania to Larenia... that's quite a big change."

"Quite. They are lovely children though, and they could do with a friend. They don't know anyone here."

"That's a wonderful idea. So the problem will stop?"

"I will make sure of it."

"Thank you so much, Mr Decker. That's a great help. I'd better be going now, anyway. Thanks again," I made my way towards the door.

"Wait a minute, Januari," I halted, and turned back to him. He gave me a look which was a mixture of stern and concerned, "how are things... at home? I know it must be hard for you. Your friends are at college, and... I would have thought you were the kind of girl who would have wanted to go to college."

"Things are fine, Mr Decker. I've got it. My friends will all go and... achieve their dreams. Genevieve with her astrophysics, Victoria with her languages, Jemima with her art, and... things are changing in my life."

"Really? In what way?"

"Well, I got a job."

"Great! Well done! What about your friends? Surely you must miss them. Are you still in contact with them?"

"Yes, I am, and I do miss them, but I have another friend, as of yesterday, and that's all I need at the moment."

"Good. I'm glad to hear you're getting on well. Just as long as you aren't working yourself too hard. Bye, Januari."

"Goodbye, Mr Decker."

I exited the room, smiling. All the teachers at Oldgate always told me not to work myself too hard. That was all I ever got from most people. I supposed they had my best interests at heart, but they should know by now that my limits weren't the same as your average 17-year-old.

I wrote another letter/diary entry that evening. It went as follows:

Dear Father,

I went to work again today. Well, obviously, that's what happens when you get a job. I spent lunchtime with Mr Derby again. I really enjoy talking to him. He seems to understand, even though he doesn't know the truth about me. I'm starting to wish I could tell him.

April is still being bullied. So I went to talk to Mr Decker (her Head of Year) about the matter this evening. He says it will get sorted, and he has some good ideas how. I'll be glad when that stops – it's been going on for too long now. I do worry about her.

I know I'll never send you these letters, but it brings me comfort just to write them, because I feel so alone. I know I have my sisters, and Mr Derby, but it's like I'm living in two different worlds.

Just as Februari and the others will never understand my work life, Mr Derby will never understand my life at home. It's as if there are two of me, each living a different life. Januari Winters and Janet Woods. I'll end up breaking in two if I'm not careful.

I'm not sure I've done the right thing. The work is fine, I've got it under control, but...it's the fact that I go by a different name and age there. I'm not me there, I'm living a lie, and... I'm not sure I can keep it up forever. I'm falling apart, and there's nothing to keep me together.

It's a good thing no one will ever read this, because the truth is everyone thinks I'm such a good person, brave and honest and smart, and I'm just not. I really wish I could be, but I'm not what everyone thinks I am. I'm just afraid that I'll do something wrong, and that I'll disappoint my sisters and my friends. That I'll fail. Really, I'm just a scared little girl trying to be something she isn't.

I just need to stick with it, and I'll get used to it. This is how I felt when I first had to look after my sisters. It will pass, with time. One thing I am is determined, and that should be enough to keep me going.

Love,

Januari

Chapter 13

Scio te quis sis

I know who you are – Latin

The next day, before breaktime, I taught a Year 11 class. That was when I realised that there was a flaw in my plan - someone from Februari's school, Ella Wright, had moved to Newgate a couple of years before, and she knew who I was. She'd used to try and pick on Februari, but Febs wasn't having any of it. Ella had been the type of person who picked on whoever she could, a lot like Kay and Kylie who targeted April because she was vulnerable. She hadn't seen me since I was in Year 10, but I hadn't changed much since then. Now she was sitting in front of me, in that class.

She stared at me. I sat her at the back of the classroom with a very tall student in front of her so she wouldn't be able to see me. Register order thankfully seemed a good enough excuse for doing this. Ella Wright didn't say anything in the lesson, but came to find me afterwards.

"All right," she said angrily, tossing her long blonde hair and marching over to me purposefully, "you're lucky I didn't say anything in the lesson."

"I'm sorry," I said, trying to sound confident and authoritative, "I don't know what you're talking about."

"Oh, really? Does the name Januari Winters not mean anything to you?"

"I've never known anyone called Januari." That was truthful enough.

"Well, you can play dumb, but I know it's you, Januari. What do you think you're doing, marching in here playing the grown-up? You're only 17. All you've ever done is play the grown-up. I'm not stupid, you know. You think you're so smart, but I can see right through you. I suppose I shouldn't be surprised."

"How dare you?! Talk to a teacher like that, I mean. Do you really think Mr Marsden would have hired a 17-year-old? If you ever talk to me like that again, it will most definitely be a detention. I suggest you get yourself out of this classroom, Miss Wright."

"Well, either you're an exceptionally good actress, or..." she shook her head, at a loss for words, "I'm sorry. I'll see you next lesson... *Miss.*"

"See you next lesson. I've got my eye on you, Eleanor Wright," I got her name wrong intentionally, hoping it would help with the act of knowing nothing of Januari Winters.

"It's Ella, and I've got my eye on you as well... Miss Woods," she left the room, glaring at me.

When she was gone, I collapsed against the wall, sighing. I seemed to have pulled it off relatively well. I knew she still had suspicions. I should have thought of this. I was just going to have to be more careful. I found myself shivering, though it wasn't cold.

I thought of what would happen if she told anyone the truth. If everyone found out my secret. Brian would surely fire me, and Mr Derby... what would he say? He'd never had a friend before, he would be absolutely shattered to find that his friend had lied to him. I imagined the hurt, bewildered, uncomprehending expression on his face. I almost burst out crying. If I lost my job, I'd fail my sisters, and I'd lose everything. Worst of all, I'd lose my friend. Everyone would look down on me, and there'd be no coming back from what I'd done.

That lunchtime, I went to the bench in the park again with Mr Derby.

"So how's your day been so far, Janet?" he inquired.

"Terrible. One of the students... knows something about me that she shouldn't, and I'm afraid she'll use it against me. She has no reason to tell anyone, but if anyone ever found out..." I shuddered, "I can't let that happen. I'm sorry... I meant: Fine, how about you?"

"The same as ever. You know, if you ever want to talk to anyone..."

"I'm fine, really. I'm sorry, I have a habit of saying too much. I can keep other people's secrets, but my own? Nope."

"Well, I hope the student doesn't tell anyone, whatever it is."

"Thank you. Mr Derby... can I ask you something?"

"Of course."

"The other day, when Brian said you never smiled, you said it was true. Why don't you smile?"

"Because there isn't anything to smile about. I've never really felt happy for ten years. Though the opposite is true too. I've never felt particularly sad in years either. It's as if my ability to feel passionate emotions has just gone. Maybe Brian's right about me."

"Don't say that; it isn't true - and I bet you can feel passionate emotions. There is always something to be happy about. Think about it. Isn't there anything you care about?"

"Yes, there are things I care about. They weren't there until recently, but they're there now."

"Think about those things. Do they not make you happy?"

"Yes, but... why are you doing this? Are you trying to make me smile?"

"I want you to be happy. Be glad for what you do have. Because you do have lots of things that I don't have."

"What do I have that you don't have?" He looked genuinely confused.

"You have the freedom to do whatever you want. You could travel the world; you could interact with other people, have a social life."

"And you don't have those things?"

"No. There is a... shall we say, *situation* at home, which prevents me from doing lots of things that I should be able to do. I should be somewhere else right now, but... I don't have a choice."

"You have things I don't have as well. What is a life without someone to share it with? I bet you have a family. Friends. People that love you, and that you love. I don't have any of that. You're my only friend. No one loves me. That's why I am the way I am. I have never had love in my life, and I am beginning to doubt I ever will."

"I'm sorry. I didn't mean..."

"It's okay. I'm used to it. My dreams... faded long ago."

"Mine too. It seems ridiculous now. The things I dreamed of seemed so simple, like something I could have one day, but it turns out that's all they were. Dreams. Desires. Things I wanted, but could never have. Don't you find that everyone wants what they can't have?"

"That's actually a very good point. I didn't really notice that before. You know, Janet, I'm really glad to have you as a friend. You're just the kind of friend I wanted when I was a child."

"I was happy as a child, and blissfully so. Like the sunshine before the storm."

"I never had that. It's just been constant storm."

I laughed, "well, I hope the storm passes over soon. If the storm's lasted so long, I bet when it passes, it will be a beautiful day."

"I hope so. I really hope so," he said, smiling.

"Mr Derby – you're smiling."

"I... I am. Janet, you did it! You found me. The real me. I've been lost for a long time, and now... I'm me again. I'm a person with passionate emotions, and... oh, it's you, you made me feel happy again. You made me smile. You did it."

"Oh no. It wasn't me. I haven't done anything. You were there all along. You had the ability to be happy all along."

He was still smiling, and it was a real smile that reached his grey eyes, which were alight with happiness. I smiled back at him.

"Janet... you don't realise how much you do for me. I've never had a friend before, and...well... shall we just say, I'm glad it's you."

I threw my arms around him, then froze suddenly, feeling awkward. Oops. He laughed, and put his arms around me.

"Sorry," I said, blushing.

"Don't worry about it. It's just... no one's ever hugged me before. I'm glad it's you, Jan."

I released him, feeling slightly less awkward. Then the bell rang, so we bade each other farewell, and went in our separate directions to teach our next lessons.

My smile faded as I walked away from him. He thought I was such a good person. If he ever found out that I was lying to him, I didn't know what he'd do. I hated lying to him. He trusted me, but I wasn't worthy of his trust. I wished I didn't have to do that, but I did.

That evening, my writings were as follows:

Dear Father,

Today one of the kids in Februari's year who moved to Newgate recognised me. Ella Wright. I think I pulled it off – just. I know she still suspects me, though, and I don't know what to do. If she told the others, I'd be sacked before I could say 'Umaro.' They would never understand. As for Mr Derby...I don't think he would ever forgive me. I really hate lying, it feels all wrong. I want to be myself, but I can't be.

I spent lunchtime with Mr Derby again, and I got him to smile. I'm so glad he's happy. I feel so cruel though, lying like this. I feel like the villain in my own story. In a way, I am, because I won't get a happy ending, but I do have Mr Derby as a friend, and I'm so glad. I don't know what I'd do without him.

Love, Januari

The next day when I arrived at work, all the teachers were standing out on the pitch.

"Good morning, Janet," said Brian, "or, should I say, Januari? Only 17, Ella tells me? You're just a child!"

Ella Wright stood beside him, looking smug. The other teachers were all whispering amongst themselves and pointing at me, sniggering. Except Mr Derby. He just stood there looking at me uncomprehendingly. Somehow, that was worse.

"Janet?" he murmured, "you lied to me?"

"She lied to us all," declared Ella dramatically. She looked at Mr Derby, grinning cruelly, "I bet she never even liked you."

"That isn't true!" I yelled. I hurried over to Mr Derby, trying to decide what to do.

"I trusted you," he whispered, "I thought you were my friend. Please, please tell me it isn't true."

I shook my head, tears of utter despair springing to my eyes, "I'm sorry. I never wanted to hurt anyone. Least of all you, Mr Derby," I looked at him, straight into his eyes, silently begging for forgiveness, "please. You're my friend."

He stepped away from me, "not any more. How do I know I can trust you? You've lost my trust, and you can never get it back. Get away from me. I don't ever want to see you again."

At that moment, my heart broke clean in two. I started crying silently.

"I suggest you get out of here, little girl," ordered Brian, smirking, "you've failed. Leave and never come back."

I turned and ran, sobbing, my head in my hands. I never wanted to come back. I wanted to run away, to leave Lilidell and never return.

I suddenly sat up straight, gasping. I looked around. I was in my bed, in my room, surrounded by my sisters who were all, miraculously, still asleep. I got up and left the room silently, not wanting to disturb my sisters.

It had all been a *dream*, I told myself. Just a stupid nightmare, but it had been so *real*... and it could, potentially, come true.

I went downstairs and made myself a hot chocolate. It was what I always did for my sisters when they had a nightmare. It usually worked.

Then again, they always had me to console them, and consoling myself wasn't going to work. This was just rubbing in the fact that I had no one. I had my sisters at home, and Mr Derby at work, but no one was constant.

I decided to spend the rest of the night on the sofa. If the nightmare came back, I didn't want to disturb my sisters. So I went to sleep thinking of work, worrying about what would happen if my secret was discovered.

Chapter 14
Tajne głęboko
A secret buried deep – Polish

Thankfully, my dream did *not* come true the next day. I woke up and did my best to forget it. I held my breath as I arrived at work, but everyone treated me completely normally, to my immense relief.

I tried to think about why Ella Wright was so cross that I was working at Newgate. It was probably just that I was only a year older than her, and she didn't like me having authority over her. So, what could I do to remedy that? I supposed the best thing would be to just carry on doing what I was doing - treating the Newgate students as equals, not as inferiors. That's how I would have wanted teachers to treat me; that's how I treated the students – fairly.

You don't need me to tell you what I did at lunchtime by this point. I spent every lunchtime the same way. I was so predictable – I amused myself sometimes.

"Janet..." said Mr Derby, "can I ask you something?"

"Of course."

"When you said yesterday that a student knew something about you that she shouldn't know, why were you so scared?"

"Because... if anyone found out, I could lose everything. My family and everyone I know would realise that I'm not as good a person as they think I am. I'd have to go home and tell my sisters that I'd failed. They'd see me for who I really am, and that isn't a good person."

"You've been keeping something from me," he guessed, "something big."

"I'm sorry. It isn't easy. I don't want to lie to you. I wish I could tell you, but I don't have a choice."

"Why not? You can trust me. You can tell me anything."

"I know, and I do trust you. It's just... like you said, it's a big thing. I'm not sure I can find the words. It's something there's no coming back from. You'd probably never want to see me again. Honestly, it's... better this way."

I really did think it was better that way. Better he knew this me, the false version of me who was a good person, like a storybook heroine, than the real me. The one who'd lied to him, despite how good he was to me, and was too afraid to tell him the truth.

As we got to know each other better, he'd want to know more about me. He'd want to know about my family, and wouldn't he find it a little strange that all my sisters were named after the months of the year and I wasn't?

Maybe I'd made the wrong decision. Maybe I couldn't have friends here. Maybe I should just... *no.* I told myself. *You made a decision, now stick with it. Admit it – you want to be his friend... and he is your friend. One of your best friends whether you like it or not.*

"Janet?" he looked at me, and I started, taken by surprise. Though I didn't know why. "Just know that... I'll always be your friend, no matter what... and this secret... if you want to tell me, then you can. If you don't... then I'll leave it alone. Whatever it is, it doesn't matter."

"Oh, I think it does. It matters a great deal, and I spend my every living moment, every sleepless night thinking about it. You can't say it makes no difference; you don't know what I've done."

"All right, I understand. So...what's your favourite book?"

It was an obvious attempt to change the topic, but I was grateful for it. So we talked about books for the rest of the time, and I relaxed. I was glad for a change of topic. It just made me realise more that this was an innocent man, an innocent man whom I'd lied to for no good reason. Surely the truth should matter more than that. I dwelt on the matter on the way home.

Because, the truth... it was something I was afraid of, something I hated the idea of anyone discovering.

Surely your friend should matter more to you than that. I thought to myself, but that was the problem. He was my friend, and I wanted it to stay that way. If I lost his trust, I could never get it back. If he found out that I'd lied to him, he'd never want to see me again.

Surely if I told him the truth, instead of him finding out, it would be proof that I trusted him. Proof that I was his friend.

He'd never had a friend before. All he'd ever had was people that deceived him, and lied to him... and I was no different. It would hurt him so much to find out that his so-called friend had lied to him. Just another of those dark shadows.

He knew I was keeping something from him. He knew that there was a big secret, and *he still seemed to want to be my friend.* If I trusted him, why could I not tell him the truth?

I was afraid of losing him. He was my friend, and that meant so much to me, but why was I so afraid of losing him? I had other friends: Genevieve, and Jemima and Victoria.

They were in Rosamontis. Mr Derby was my only friend at the moment, and that was why it meant so much to me.

I didn't even know his first name. That was because no one called him by his first name! It was a reminder of his past which he quite clearly did not wish to discuss. I was different, I was his friend. No, I wasn't any different from anyone else. I'd lied to him!

I was overthinking this, and I needed to stop thinking about it right now before I started coming to ridiculous conclusions like... no. That was unthinkable. I couldn't even let that thought cross my mind. There was no way that... *stop.* I told myself.

Januari Winters, you need to calm down and start thinking about something else. This subject is forbidden. It's the end of the day, now. Go home, and not another thought about anything vaguely related to this topic. Think about... anything else. Like what's for tea tonight or what you're going to say to your sisters when you get home.

I was infuriated with myself for even letting that thought cross my mind. It was ridiculous. I seriously needed to calm myself down and think about something else.

I decided I could cook tea that night. I was tired, so I'd just do something simple like gnocchi or pasta.

Yes, gnocchi seemed a good idea. I knew we had some in, and some sauce. That would do just fine.

I wondered what my sisters had been doing at school that day. Augusta would, no doubt, come home brandishing another picture at me. I was so proud of her. Of them all. I loved my sisters. I would do anything for them.

When I got home, I did everything just as I'd planned it. Then I sat down and put a film on – Rapensela. I knew it was September's favourite, and I hoped it would help me relax. I tried to focus completely on the film and only the film.

My sisters, at least, enjoyed the film. When they were all in bed, I went downstairs, sat on the sofa and wept. I wept because I was a bad person and I didn't want to be, because I'd lied to my friend and I wanted to tell him the truth. Because I couldn't give my sisters the lives they deserved. Because I was just an insignificant 17-year-old girl, and I'd somehow managed to turn my life into a huge mess. I wrote my diary letter thing again that evening:

Dear Father,

I've made a mess out of everything. I should never have done this. I can't live with the fact that I lied to my friend. Mr Derby knows I'm keeping something from him, and he knows it's something big. I'm afraid. I want to tell him but I can't. Earlier I thought something that I can't allow myself to think. I need something to distract me. I can't live like this for much longer.

I can't believe I've made such a mess out of everything. I've lied to my friend, and I want to tell him the truth. I can't give my sisters the life they deserve. I can't seem to get anything right.

I know I just need to keep thinking positively. I can do this. I have everything under control. There's no need to worry about anything. I worry too much. I always have. I just need to keep going. I'll get used to this way of living, and everything will settle down.

I know I have a good reason for doing this, and it will benefit my sisters in the long run, which is what I want. I want them to live happily ever after, but my problem is, I don't want to hurt Mr Derby. He's my friend, and if he finds out the truth, he'll be so upset. The one person he trusts and she's deceiving him. I don't know what to do.

I wish I had someone to give me advice on what to do, but I don't. I'm on my own for this one, and I just have to hope it will work out somehow.

Love, Januari

Chapter 15

Uma luz na escuridão

A light in the darkness –Portuguese

The next day, Februari came to talk to me before I left for work.

"Just a minute, Jan," she said, grabbing my arm, "I want to talk to you."

"Okay. What is it?"

"Well... you've been kind of distant lately."

"I'm sorry."

"No, it isn't your fault, but I heard you crying last night. Are you sure this isn't too much for you?"

"I'm sorry, I'll try to cry more quietly next time," I teased.

"There won't be a next time," she said fiercely, "because whatever you were upset about, it isn't going to be a problem any more. Why were you crying?"

"I just... I hate lying to Mr Derby, and I feel like I can't do anything right at the moment. Besides, remember Ella Wright? She's in my Citanian class, and she recognised me. So if she tells anyone... well, I'm screwed, aren't I?"

"You've mentioned this 'Mr Derby' quite a lot over the past few days. Who is he?"

"He's a Larenian teacher, and he's my friend. I like to spend my lunchtimes with him, in the park. I feel like he understands me. It's weird, I know, but he's my friend, and I wish I didn't have to lie to him."

"Maybe you don't have to."

"Febs, face it. If I told him the truth, he'd never forgive me for lying to him. I made a mistake, and now I have to pay the price. I just have to make sure my secret stays nice and... well... secret. I have to go, I'll see you when I get back. I love you, Febs."

"I love you too, Januari. We all do. Never forget that. No matter what happens, we'll always be there for you."

I grabbed June, July, Augusta, September, Octoba, November and December (not literally) and rushed out of the door. I was running late. I somehow still managed to make it to work on time.

Later, I went to the park with Mr Derby.

"Hello, Mr Derby," I greeted him.

"Janet... call me Amycus."

"Amycus?"

"Yes. That's my name. I never really liked it much, but... my friend should at least call me by my first name. So I would prefer for you to call me Amycus from now on, before you get into the habit of calling me Mr Derby."

"...Okay. Amycus, then."

"I want to tell you about my childhood. What I was like growing up. How I became so distant and cold-hearted."

"You aren't cold-hearted. Don't say that about yourself. You aren't like that. You're kind, and intelligent, and... you're my friend."

He smiled gratefully, "perhaps my heart isn't cold now, but it used to be. I don't want to bore you, if you would rather talk about something else...?"

"No, I'm listening."

"Okay. Well, I never knew anything about my family, but I was brought up in an orphanage, so I assumed my parents were dead. So no family, for starters.

The other kids at the orphanage... well, I was different from all the others. I loved to read, and they were all idiots. A few of them there were Jake Barker, Abigail White and Benjamin Smith.

I never had any friends, so they started to tease me. The boy whose name means friend, but didn't have any friends, and they called me... Friendless. That's what everyone called me, and they thought nothing of it. 'Friendless, can you pass me the glue?' 'Hi, Friendless, how are you doing?' They never once stopped to think about what it meant, and how it made me feel every time I heard someone call me that.

The more decent of them called me 'Derby', and all my teachers called me 'Derby'. Not one person ever called me by my first name.

All the other kids at the orphanage... well, the boys all acted like three-year-olds. They were all idiots and mucked around all the time. The girls were all your stereotypical popular teenage girls. Loved dancing and make-up and boys... so, as you can imagine, I was on my own.

Seeing me suffer always gave Jake great pleasure, especially if he was the one causing me pain. He always took away everything I cared about, and my notebook... in which I confided my deepest secrets, my burning desires and my dreams... he took it and showed it to everyone at the orphanage, and they teased me more.

I used to dream that maybe, one day, someone would care about me. I dreamed of finding true love, but... I never even had any friends, and I gave up on that dream when I was 15.

It was the fact that I was without love that made me so... distant from everyone else. No one ever loved me, and I never loved anyone, because no one was ever kind to me, no one ever...I never made any difference to anyone. I don't really matter to anyone, and nothing's changed.

I've thought for a long time that my story won't have a happy ending. That I'll be forever alone. That was my greatest fear – being alone. I feared that it would be that way for the rest of my life.

That's why finally having a friend meant so much to me – because it means I'm not alone. I have a friend, at least, and that's why, if you decide at some point that you want to tell me your secret, I'll still be your friend. I'll always be here if you need me, and if you want to talk to someone... I hope you'll think of me as someone you can trust."

"Amycus... thank you for telling me that. It must be hard talking about your childhood and... I'll always want to be your friend. When you realise what a bad person I am, and tell me you never want to see me again, just know that I'll still be here if you need me. I'm definitely not going anywhere, not that I have a choice, but it means a lot that you told me that. If you ever want to talk to someone... you can trust me."

"Thank you, Janet. I just needed to tell someone. I don't have anyone to talk to except you, so... thank you for listening."

"Amycus... I will tell you my secret. At some point. When I'm ready, but I promise you that I will tell you... and I do trust you."

"I know, but I'm not going to make you promise that. You can change your mind if you want to. You don't have to tell me if you think... if you think it is better I don't know."

"I'm just afraid... that the truth will hurt you. That you wouldn't think of me in the same way. So my secret stays secret for now, but... I will probably tell you at some point. I'll tell you this much; I'm not as good a person as you think I am. I do not deserve to be your friend, and I am no different to anyone else you've met."

"That isn't true. As long as this person I know is the real you, you are a good person. You are my friend, and for good reasons too. You are different to everyone else I've met before. You're one in a million, Janet Woods. You're kind, and brave, and hardworking. Everyone else I've met... all other people do is deceive me. You... you're different, and I trust you. You're my friend, Janet."

When I was walking home, I felt absolutely awful. Amycus had just told me so much about himself, and he didn't even know my real name. He had me all wrong. The person he knew wasn't the real me. It was just a fake person hiding behind a mask of someone who didn't really exist.

I hated lying to him. I knew I was going to have to tell him the truth at some point. Or he'd find out for himself, what with my Ella Wright dilemma, and I had much rather tell him myself than have Ella

Wright reveal my secret to everyone. Then at least he'd know I trusted him.

That evening, I wrote:

Dear Father,

This doesn't seem to be getting any better. Today Mr Derby told me about his childhood. I call him by his first name now – Amycus. He trusted me with so much information about himself, and yet he doesn't even know my real name. I feel awful.

I know now that his discovering the truth is inevitable, really, but it depends how it happens – either I tell him or he finds out another way, and I know which one I'd prefer. I need to somehow find the words to tell him everything. I don't know what I'm going to do.

He means a lot to me. He's one of my best friends. I can't keep lying to him like this. Yesterday, that thing I thought... ~~for a second I thought I was falling in love with him.~~ I can't allow myself to even consider that possibility. If that unthinkable thing happened... I would just end up falling apart.

Anyway... we're just friends. Nothing more. I'm just going to have to be stricter with myself. I'm not sure what, but... I have to do something. I'll work something out. I'm hardly sleeping at all at the moment. When I do sleep, I just have the same recurring nightmare about being exposed for what I've done. Losing everything, and running away knowing that I'd failed, and it echoes in my head.

I'm just so afraid that if I tell him... well, I don't want to hurt him. I need to talk to someone, but there's no one to talk to. Just myself. At times like this, I wish I had a parent instead of having to take the place of the parent myself.

I don't know what to do with myself. I suppose it feels like I'm confiding in my father when I write this. My father before he was ill, before everything changed forever. I honestly have no idea where my future is going to go now, and... this isn't what I expected.

Love, Januari

Chapter 16
MOCT 1
The Bridge 1 – Russian

The weeks passed slowly, and before long it was nearly the end of the term. It had been the end of February when I'd started working at Newgate, and now it was almost Easter. During those weeks I'd spent at Newgate, Amycus had become one of my best friends.

I never tired of talking to him, and he always seemed to know exactly what to say to me in every situation. At that point, there was no one I'd rather spend time with than Amycus, and he knew me just as well as Jemima, Victoria and Genevieve.

One day in the penultimate week of term, when I got back from work, Februari was bursting to talk to me.

"Jan, Alfie asked me out! This Saturday evening, I'm meeting him at 8pm at The Fox's Den. That will be all right, won't it? I can't believe it!"

"Yes, that's fine... if it's what you really want. I wasn't into that whole boyfriend thing, but I'm really pleased that you're happy. I have to warn you, though. Amycus knows his brother, and if he's anything like him... well, I'll give him a chance, of course. For you. Just... don't stay out too late on Saturday night, okay?"

"Thanks, Jan! You're the best. It will be fine, I promise."

"Good luck."

It wasn't long before Saturday came, and it was the day of Februari's first date. I was exhausted after my first term of work, and I was very glad that it was finally the weekend.

That afternoon, I had a sudden thought – wouldn't it be better if Mum had a friend? Because, at the moment, she was alone in her suffering. She rarely talked to my sisters or me. She spent most of her time either at work, or at the hospital with Father. I knew how she must be feeling.

I remembered she'd had a very close friend – Amanda Thatcher – when she was younger, but had let her go during college. If I remembered correctly, we still had her phone number somewhere.

So, after much searching, I eventually found it in one of the sideboard drawers. I thought it best not to consult Mum about this. I was doing what was best for her. I picked up the house phone and dialled the number, then I waited, with baited breath.

"Hello?" answered a voice on the other end of the phone, "Amanda Curtis speaking." *Amanda Curtis*, I thought. *She must be married now.*

"Did you used to be Amanda Thatcher?"

"Yes, I did... but I've been married a long time now. You must know me from a long time ago."

"I don't know you, but my mum does – please don't hang up!"

"Who's speaking, please?"

"My name is Januari Winters."

"Winters? Like Jack Winters?"

"Yes. He's my father."

"And who's your mum?"

"Summer."

"Summer's daughter," she replied flatly.

"Yes, that's right."

"Then I have no interest in talking to you."

"Please don't hang up, Amanda! Please?"

"All right, Winters, get to the point. What do you want?"

"Well, here's the thing-"

"Why are you contacting me now? I haven't seen Summer in over 20 years. She let me go. I even tried to call Elise, but there was no answer."

"Elise?"

"Yes, she's a good person... how is she?"

I hadn't realised that Amanda didn't know about Elise. I pondered for a second how best to tell her this information. Then I quietly informed her, "she's dead. There was a car crash while Summer was at university."

"I'm sorry to hear that. Elise... was really lovely."

"I never knew her... but, as I was saying, my father – Jack – has been in hospital with cancer for seven years. He was diagnosed eight years ago and... you know how much he meant to Summer. She just couldn't do it any more. My sisters... I have to look after them, and I make all the decisions and things.

I don't know why I didn't think of this before, but... she needs you. I understand completely, it must be so hard for her. I know you'll be afraid to make contact again, and probably cross with her for shutting you out, but... she's still the same person you once knew, inside. She needs you, even if she doesn't know it.

So if you wanted to come round sometime, you have our number now. I don't want to be pushy or anything, but I'm doing this for her – Amanda?"

"...I would love to see Summer again," she said hastily, "I'd love to meet you. If I could come round sometime, Victor – my husband – could watch the kids, and... I'd see my friend again. When would be best for you? What time?"

"On a weekend or something, or after school sometime... you could come round tomorrow if you like."

"Tomorrow? Would you be okay with that?"

"Sure, I just... Mum needs a friend right now. How does... 2:30 pm tomorrow sound to you?"

"Perfect. Then it's settled."

"Great! Our address is 11, Oldgate Road, Oldgate, West Golding, Lilidell, 3LI6JS."

"Thanks. Got it. How old are you, Januari?"

"17."

"Only 17? And you organise... everything? Shouldn't you be at college?"

"I can't go to college. My sisters need me here. I'll see you tomorrow, Amanda."

"Okay, bye."

I sighed and put the phone down, satisfied. It would be a nice surprise for Mum. She'd be so glad to see her friend again. It was also a subtle reminder that her daughters were here for her if she needed us as well.

That evening, Februari went out. She was, needless to say, very excited about her first date. I told her to be careful, and not to be out too late, because after hearing more about Alfie's brother, I wasn't getting an overly good first impression. I hoped for Februari's sake that Alfie was nothing like Jake.

I wished her luck, and reminded her of what I'd said before. She beamed, and then she was gone. I sat, waiting for her to return. December's bedtime passed. Then November's. Then September and Octoba's. Then June, July and Augusta's. Then March, April and May's. Then Februari's.

The time I usually went to bed was 10:00. I thought I'd give Februari some time. She was probably just enjoying herself, but by the time 11:00 came, I was starting to get seriously worried. What if something had happened to her? By 11:30, I was just about to get up and leave when my phone rang.

I had my own mobile phone – Mum's old one. I didn't really use it much, but kept it on and charged in case of emergency. I'd been using it to keep in contact with my friends.

It wasn't a familiar number, but I picked it up immediately.

"Hello?"

"Hi, it's me. Febs."

"Febs! Where do you think you've been? I've been going out of my mind with worry! Where are you? What happened? Are you all right?"

"Slow down a minute. I'm sorry. Really, but you were right about Alfie. He didn't like me for me, he only wanted... a physical relationship, and I refused, so he showed his true colours. He said he only wanted to go out with me because he thought I was pretty. I'm not sure I can get myself home."

Her voice was full of emotion, and she was clearly crying.

"Oh, Febs. I'm so sorry. I'll come now, I'll come and find you. I'll help you get home, and I think hot chocolate is in order."

"Thank you. You're a life-saver. I love you. I'm so glad you're my sister. I don't know what I'd do without you."

"I'll see you soon, Februari. I love you too, and don't you forget that. I'll be there as soon as I can."

"I'll see you soon. Okay, bye."

I had my coat on and was out of the door almost before she'd even hung up.

The place Februari was at was this kind of hang-out place, called 'The Fox's Den.' It served drinks, and it was somewhere you went to socialize, somewhere you went to sit and talk for long periods of time. I'd never been, but it had a reputation for being the favourite place to meet and socialize for most teenagers and young people.

I opened the door and looked around. I saw Febs curled up in the corner.

"Februari!" I called, and I ran across the room to where she was, and I threw my arms around her.

"Oh, Jannie, I'm so sorry, I should never have got into this sort of thing," she sobbed.

"It's okay, Februari. Jannie's here. I've got you. Let's get you home, and I'll make a nice mug of hot chocolate, and then... I'll sing you my lullaby to help you get to sleep, yes?"

"I love you, Jan."

"I love you too, Februari. Just remember – none of this was your fault. Alfie Barker must have serious problems."

"Jan, someone you know helped me, after Alfie... and he let me borrow his phone to call you. Look behind you."

I turned, and to my great surprise saw Amycus standing there.

"Amycus! What are you doing here?"

"I was just trying to help Februari. She looked like she needed help. I didn't know she was your sister."

"You helped my sister. Thank you."

"You're welcome. I'm here with a group of people from the orphanage where I grew up."

"I thought you didn't like the people there...?"

"They've changed. They're all right, I suppose. I was just trying to be polite. They were probably only inviting me to be nice... will Februari be okay?"

"She will be, I hope. She had a situation. I can't relate, but she'll get through it. She's strong."

"Do you know what happened?"

"Yes. She was here with Jake's brother, Alfie. She really liked him; she was thrilled when he asked her out, but... he didn't like her for her, he only wanted... and she refused. So then he said what he really thought about her, and... well... you can guess what happened then. She was heartbroken. I've never been in that kind of relationship with anyone."

"Have you ever been in love?"

"Oh, no. No one would want me. I have no social life and I have nothing to give."

"Oh, I think you do. You're beautiful, intelligent, hardworking, brave, determined... I could make a list a mile long."

I looked at him, touched. He was probably just saying that to make me feel better, but even so... "You really think so?"

"Yes, that's what I think."

"Well... even if that was the case, which it isn't, the person would eventually realise that they'd be better off without me. They'd just get burdened with all my problems."

He took my hands and looked at me. His eyes were gentle, sympathetic, kind. "You don't need to worry," he told me, "about anything, and... I'll always be here for you if you need me. You can rely on me, you can trust me."

"I know," I said softly, "thank you, Amycus." There was a moment's silence, and then I was jerked back into reality.

"Well, I need to be getting Februari home. It's late."

"Okay. I'll see you on Monday, Januari."

I suddenly realised I still had hold of his hands, and let them go hastily. I smiled at him, "goodbye, Amycus. It was really nice to see you."

I leaned up and kissed him on the cheek quickly. I hadn't meant to, it just sort of happened. *What was wrong with me?* It made me suddenly realise – I was helplessly in love with Amycus Derby, and there was nothing I could do about it. I smiled at him again, and he smiled back. Then I took Februari's hand, and we left for home without saying another word.

Chapter 17
MOCT 2
The Bridge 2 – Russian

Later that night – or, should I say, early the next morning – I went out for a walk in the starlight. It was something I hadn't done for a while, and it helped to clear my mind. As I'd just realised I was in love with my friend, I needed to clear my mind.

There was a hilly walk in between Oldgate and Newgate, about 5 kime, which cut down into the woods. It was a clear night, which meant I could see the stars. They truly were the most incomprehensibly beautiful thing in existence. Yet it reminded me painfully of Genevieve. Usually, I never came across anyone else.

Tonight was different. About halfway through the walk, I saw a group of young men standing over another young man. One of them was holding a knife. As I got closer, I realised that the man on the ground was Amycus, and the blond one with the knife I assumed must be Jake Barker as he looked just like an older Alfie. What a coincidence.

Jake and the others were clearly drunk. "No one cares about you," I heard Jake saying, "if I killed you, it wouldn't make any difference to anyone." I was furious. How dare they talk to Amycus like that? He just seemed to be cowering on the floor, unable to do anything. He was shaking.

I wanted to do something, but I didn't want Amycus to know it was me. I saw Jake raise the knife.

Reacting instinctively, I put up my hood, hoping that would be enough to keep them from seeing my face, and leapt at Jake. I pushed him to the ground, getting him away from Amycus. He scrambled to his feet and backed away from me.

"Get away," I commanded, "go on. Leave him alone. All of you. If you hurt him, you will have to answer to me."

They did as I said, wandering off somewhere else. I wondered why Jake had had a knife with him... I decided not to dwell on the matter too much.

Amycus got to his feet, wincing. He looked at me. "You saved my life. Thank you," he said.

"You're welcome."

"Who are you?"

"Never mind that. Come with me."

I led him to the woods, where I started a fire (I was practiced at this, as I used to love going camping with Victoria, Genevieve and Jemima. I still had some matches in my coat pocket from the last time we did this.)

"Can I at least see the face of the girl who saved my life?" he asked.

"No. I'm sorry, that would give me away."

"Well, I should introduce myself, at least. My name is Amycus Derby."

"I know."

"You know? But... how much more do you know about me?"

"Your name is Amycus Derby, you're 22 years old. You work as a Larenian teacher at Newgate High School. You were brought up in an orphanage."

"How do you... are you some kind of angel?"

"I am no angel, I promise you."

"Well... do you know Janet Woods?"

"One might say that, yes."

"Don't tell me her secret or anything, but can you tell me something?"

"How do you know you can trust me?"

"I just get a feeling... anyway, I accidentally called her Januari earlier, and she didn't seem to notice my calling her by the wrong name."

"You called her *what?!*"

"Januari. I don't know why. I don't know anyone else called Januari, obviously, but... I had a dream once that I'd meet... someone... called Januari, and I was thinking about it."

"Well... it's similar to her name, and she was thinking about something else, so... maybe that's why she didn't notice."

"Yes..."

"I should also tell you... her secret... she isn't telling you, because she cares about you. She's afraid it will hurt you, and she doesn't want to lose your friendship."

"Whatever it is... I would forgive her."

"No... she isn't who you think she is. She's lying to you, and she hates it. She wants more than anything to tell you the truth, but she can't. She's afraid, because she isn't any different to anyone else you've met. They all lie to you and deceive you, and she's deceiving you too, but she wishes she didn't have to."

"That's what makes all the difference. So I would still forgive her. I trust that she has a good reason for doing so. How do you know that, anyway? Who are you? Can you at least tell me your name?"

"It's Januari. Now listen to me for a minute: you are not alone, and nor are you unloved. Remember that, Amycus."

"Will I see you again, Januari?"

"You will, but you won't know it's me. I have to go. Goodbye, Amycus Derby."

I hurried off into the woods, in the direction of home, taking my hood down as I got further away from him. It had been a long day. After that first week, I'd stopped writing to Father but now, what with all that had happened, I felt I needed to write another letter before I went to sleep.

Dear Father,

It's been weeks since I started working at Newgate. Nothing much has changed, but Amycus is one of my best friends now, and I don't know what I'd do without him.

Today Februari went on a date with Alfie Barker, at The Fox's Den. It went awfully; she certainly won't be doing that again any time soon, and Amycus was there, and I've just realised – I think I love him.

But I'm afraid. I don't want to talk to anyone about it, I just want to get rid of these feelings before it's too late. My reasons are:

1) He would never think about me like that,

2) I'll just end up with a broken heart, and
3) He's my friend, and I can't let myself think about him like that.

I can't afford to go falling in love, so I'm not going to talk to Februari or anyone about it because that makes it more real. If I can fall in love so easily, after only knowing someone for such a short time, then it shouldn't be that hard to make myself fall out of love. I have to. I have no choice.

Love, Januari

As planned, Amanda Thatcher-now-Curtis came round on Sunday afternoon. When she arrived, I greeted her and invited her in. Then I went upstairs to get Mum. I went into her room where she sat, staring blankly at the wall.

"Mum?" I said gently, "there's someone here to see you."

"Whoever it is, I don't care. I don't want to see anyone," she replied tonelessly.

"I think you do. Just come with me. Please? I organised for her to come round especially for you. It isn't us she's here to see."

"All right, then, fine."

She followed me downstairs, and into the living room. Then she stopped, seeing Amanda.

"Amanda," she whispered, "Amanda Thatcher."

Amanda smiled uncertainly, "hello, Summer."

My mum ran over and threw her arms around her friend. I was so glad to see her somewhere remotely near happy again.

Amanda stayed for the rest of the afternoon, and set off for home shortly after tea. We organised for her to come again two weeks later. As she left, she turned and said to Mum:

"I hope you realise what an amazing daughter you have. Not every 17-year-old would put up with what your Januari puts up with. You should be very proud."

Mum said nothing, but waved Amanda off. When she was gone, Mum came over to me. "Januari... Amanda's right, you know," she said, "most 17-year-olds wouldn't have the ability, or maturity, or... selflessness, to take on what you live with every day. I'm sorry about... everything, but I'm not sure I could... you look after them better than me. I am proud of you, Jan."

"I just wanted to make you happy, Mum," I replied.

"There's no need to be modest."

"I'm not being modest so much as stating things as they are."

"In your eyes, Januari. In your eyes. There's something else I have to ask you about, anyway."

"What is it, Mum?"

"Well... July says that you've been talking about someone called Amycus a lot recently."

I sighed, "I'm sorry."

"Who is he, exactly?"

"He's one of my best friends."

"I see. Are you sure you're just friends?"

"Yes. Definitely."

"Jan... July said you have a job now. That this 'Amycus' is a work colleague."

"That's true, but it's nothing I can't handle. Don't worry about it, Mum."

"I'm just worried that... you need to be careful, Januari, or else you'll end up falling in love. Love is dangerous. It causes pain. I don't want you getting hurt. You need to be careful. I just have to warn you... if you really must work, Jan, then I'd strongly urge you to remain focused on the job. You can't afford any... distractions."

"You're right. I've been stupid. I shouldn't... don't worry, Mum. I know nothing will come of it. He doesn't think of me in that way. Nor can I let myself think of him in that way."

"So you're really just friends?"

"Yes."

"If he wanted to be something more, would you...?" Before I could stop it, the thought came into my head of kissing Amycus, holding him close, my lips on his... no. I pushed it away. *No.* I told myself. *Don't even think about it. That could never happen, but* still...

"Well... if there was a chance that we could be happy together..."

"Januari. You can't let yourself be distracted by him. No matter how charming he may seem, whatever way he might look at you, whatever things he may say to you, romance isn't a good idea."

"I know," I blushed, "It isn't like that. Amycus is just a friend."

I went upstairs and flung myself onto my bed, furious with myself for even letting myself think that, but still... I did love him, whether I wanted to or not.

I hit my pillow angrily, not knowing what to do. "Oh, Amycus," I murmured, "I love you, I love you."

"Oh, really?" said Augusta's voice amusedly.

I sat up, shocked. "Augusta! I'm sorry, I..."

"Jannie," she said, "have you got a *boyfriend?*"

"What? No, of course not!"

"Well, who's Amycus, then?"

"My friend," I went bright red, "look, Augusta, don't tell anyone, okay? Nothing's going to happen. Really, we're just friends."

"Okay. What does he look like?"

"He has dark brown hair and grey eyes, and he has a really lovely smile. He's quite tall, and-" I stopped abruptly, "why?"

"Just curious," she smiled, "I won't say anything."

"Good," I sighed, relieved, "sorry, Augusta."

Amanda came around to visit often after that. She always found something to talk about with Mum, just like I did, just to keep her with us and try and return a sense of normalcy to her life. Sometimes when Amanda was there, I even caught her smiling, and I hadn't seen her smiling in ages. I was glad I'd been able to do something.

That evening, I wrote:

Dear Father,

It finally feels like I'm doing something useful. Today, Amanda Thatcher (well, Curtis, but close enough) came round to see Mum.

It helped take my mind off things, and Mum was happy. She was happy, Father. I know you would be proud of me. I'm finally doing something right.

I'm just glad that Mum's happy, and that I was able to do something, at least, to help her.

Tomorrow, I have to go back to work. I have to do something about my... dilemma. I'm not precisely sure what, but I'll think of something.

Love, Januari

Chapter 18
Aislingean
Dreams – Gaelic

The next day, I went back to my new weekly routine. I took June, July, Augusta, September and Octoba to school first.

When I dropped off the younger ones, Mr Mills came over to say hello.

"How are you, Jan?" he asked.

"I'm fine. I'm in a bit of a rush."

"Yes, I did notice that you seem to be in more of a hurry than normal at the moment. Why is that?"

"I got a job. I need to be there early."

"What kind of job?"

"One well suited to me. I can't really say. I'm sorry, I just... never mind."

"How's it going at the moment?"

"Very well. I have a friend there. He helps me get through it."

"Well, I'll let you get on your way. Goodbye, Jan. Look after yourself."

"Of course. It's fine; everything's under control."

I walked away, carrying December and holding November's hand. I needed to get them to nursery next. "Everything is not under control," I muttered to myself as I headed for nursery.

"What's your friend like, Jannie?" piped up November.

"He's... very intelligent, and kind, and I feel like he understands me. He's a very good friend. His name is Amycus Derby."

"Do you love him?"

"Shhhh!" I said hurriedly, "that isn't the way things work, November. He's my friend. I can't allow myself to feel like that. No one will ever think about me like that." I was talking more to myself than to her but she immediately contradicted me.

"Yes, they will. You're like... princess. You're pretty, and you're good at everything, but you say you're not. You're busy a lot. Princesses always find their Prince Charming."

"I'm afraid it's a lot more complicated than that. That isn't how things work. You're only little; you wouldn't understand. You're going to be just like a fairytale princess and one day, you'll live happily ever after, but I won't."

"Why not, Jannie?"

"Because I'm not a good person. I've lied to someone I care about. I did it because I wanted a better life for you, and the rest of our sisters. I gave up everything for you, so that your stories can have happy endings."

"I love you, Jannie. You're good. I think your dreams will come true."

"I love you too, November, but it's extremely unlikely that either of my dreams will come true."

By this point, we'd arrived at the nursery. I opened the door, and dropped off November and December.

"Hey, Jan."

"Hi, Ani. I'm sorry, I really need to go. I'm going to be late for work."

"Okay. I'm getting a bit worried about you, you know. All this rushing around... you'll exhaust yourself. You'll make yourself ill."

"I appreciate the concern, but I'm fine. Hard work is what I'm used to. Really, Ani, I have to go."

"Well, all right... take care of yourself, kid."

"I'm getting a bit old for you to be calling me that. I'll be 18 in January."

"Yeah, and I'll stop when you're legally an adult, but now, you're still only 17. So, I'll see you later, kid."

I laughed, "See you later, Oriana."

"Oy!"

"Treat others as you would have them treat you. You call me names I don't like; don't be surprised when the same happens to you," I called after her.

I left the nursery, smiling. I glanced at my watch. "Damn, I really am going to be late." I started running, as fast as I could. I was used to running, because I was constantly in a rush. I was so used to it that I rarely got out of breath any more.

I ran all the way there. I was teaching a Year 10 Citanian class first. Thankfully, I was there on time, and with some time to prepare for the lesson as well.

At lunchtime, I ended up with Amycus again. Despite exerting my best efforts to keep myself away, I couldn't do it. I thought that maybe, if I wasn't spending time with him, it would help me to get rid of these feelings before something bad happened.

These lunchtimes spent with my friend were precious to me. They were what kept me going during my work hours, something to look forward to during the morning, and dwell on throughout the afternoon, and falling out of love was proving to be extremely hard and frustrating.

I told myself I had to find something else to do that day, like read my book, but then Amycus came into the room, and my heart wouldn't let me do what I should have done. So my lunchtime on that Monday was spent like all the others.

"So how are you doing today, Janet? You seem... pensive. What are you thinking about? Is something bothering you?"

"A conversation I had with my little sister this morning."

"Februari?"

"No. Febs isn't really little any more. My sister November. She's three. Her grasp of language, I must say, is very sophisticated for a three-year-old."

"What were you talking about?"

"She still has that optimism that little children have. She was insisting that my dreams will come true, God bless her. I know they won't, but she seemed to have me mistaken for a fairytale princess."

"Why do you think your dreams won't come true?" he wondered aloud.

"It just wouldn't work," I glanced down at my feet.

"I know that feeling. I used to dream about finding true love... how ridiculous does that sound? I've given up on that dream. I mean, look at me now. Who could ever love this?"

"It doesn't sound ridiculous at all," I looked back up at him as I spoke, "there are lots of things... you're a genuinely nice person. You're kind, clever, sincere... and constant. One day, you'll fall in love, and live happily ever after. If you haven't forgotten me by then, I'll be there to say, 'I told you so.'"

"I couldn't possibly forget you, Jan... and thank you for saying that."

"I didn't technically say the word 'that'."

He laughed, "oh, you know what I mean. So what did you used to dream about?"

"I used to dream about... finding true love, as well. I know, no one would ever think about me like that. I'm just an ordinary girl. Completely average, and it's just the realisation... that I won't get a happy ending. Everyone else gets to grow up and fall in love, and I get left behind."

There were several reasons why this was not a good topic of discussion with this particular person. One was that I was talking about love with the man I was in love with, and that was never a good combination. Especially as I was trying to get rid of those feelings.

Another was that if I wasn't careful, I was going to end up saying too much about my real self, and then he'd be one step further down the path to discovering my secret. I decided to swiftly change the subject.

"I also used to dream of travelling the world. Of leaving the country and going... somewhere else. Just to escape for a little bit, to somewhere I've never been before. Like Oppidum Leo. Or... just something different, but that won't happen either. I will never be free to travel to my heart's content. I have to stay here. Both my dreams... they might have been possible once, but they aren't now."

"I'm sorry, Jan. I wish there was something I could do."

"It's okay. I gave up on those dreams a long time ago. I didn't think travelling the world was that much of an expectation, but... clearly, ordinary girls like me who give up everything for the people they love don't get happy endings."

His hand found mine, and he held it tight. He looked at me, his grey eyes piercing my brown ones.

"Janet Woods, there is nothing ordinary about you. You're the best person I've ever met. I admit, that isn't saying much, but... it's true."

"Thank you, Amycus. That means a lot."

He continued to look at me, his expression gentle and understanding.

"I know exactly how you feel, but trust me when I say that you will find true love. Whoever you give your heart to, he's the luckiest man in the world, and he'd have to be completely mad to say no to you."

I looked at him. My heart was beating about ten times its usual pace.

"No, he'd have to be mad to think about me in that way. No one would... anyway, you're probably just saying that to make me feel better."

"No, I really mean it. I'm the one who has no chance whatsoever."

"That's where you're wrong. Whoever holds your heart is the luckiest girl in the world. Though she'd have to be something pretty special to deserve that."

He smiled. I wished I'd had the courage to tell him how I felt about him, but I didn't, and I doubted I ever would. When I got back that afternoon, Augusta came straight over to me.

"Jannie! I drew you a picture," she handed it to me, beaming.

I looked at it, and gasped. She'd drawn two people, clearly meant to be me and Amycus, together, with a red heart around them. "Augusta..."

Her face fell, "Don't you like it?"

"No, it's lovely. You're very good at art, Augusta, but..." I dropped my voice to a whisper, "try to leave him out of it in future, okay?"

She nodded solemnly, "okay. I'm sorry, Jannie."

"Don't apologise. It isn't your fault." I folded it up and tucked it into my pocket.

That evening, I wrote to Father again.

Dear Father,

This isn't getting any easier. I can't cope with this much longer. Today I was talking to Amycus about dreams, and you know what I used to dream about.

He said whoever I give my heart to is the luckiest man in the world, and would be mad to say no to me. It made me feel so hopeless because I know that I can't come back from this. From any of it. I lied to him, and then I fell in love with him. I disgust myself. I don't even deserve him as a friend, let alone anything else.

I don't seem to be able to do anything about this. I need help, but I don't know who to turn to, and talking about it makes it more real.

I'm so afraid. What I really need to admit to myself is that I'm afraid of falling in love because I'll end up with a broken heart, I'll lose everything. Then I won't be able to look after my sisters properly, and I have to put them first.

I don't know what to do, Father. I've never felt so helpless in my life. Everything seems to be spinning out of control, and if I've lost control, then all I need to do is get a stronger grip. I need to be strict with myself. I need to get hold of myself. I need to be calm, and think clearly.

I need to make myself act like his friend and nothing more. Maybe then, I'll stop wanting to be more than friends. Just friends. Nothing more. I need to keep getting that into my head, because I've only known him for a term. One term. So given a bit more time, I can regain control of my life. I'll carry on going. This will sort itself out.

Or… maybe I'm not the one who needs to be in control. Maybe… I need to think to myself, what would my father say if I could really talk to him about all of this? And I know exactly what that is. You'd tell me you were proud of me, and that praying would help. Thank you, Father.

I know you would also say that I should follow my heart, but I can't. I need to think about this logically. I can't do what my heart is telling me; that would be very bad.

I'm constantly at war with myself, heart versus mind. Januari Winters versus Janet Woods, and I need to be one person, not two. I need to tell him the truth, and soon, because otherwise I'll just end up falling apart.

Love, Januari

When I'd finished writing, I said a silent prayer. God, I prayed, *let all this work out. Let everything work out for the best, and let me be able to give my sisters the lives they deserve. Amen.*

Chapter 19

Esperanzas de heredar

Expectations – Spanish

The next day, things got slightly better. I went to work, and the day went normally enough. However when I was on my way to work walking near the edge of Oldgate, an unfamiliar voice called across to me: "Hey!"

I turned. A woman stood there. She had long wavy blonde hair and glasses. She was beautiful. She hurried over to me, "you're Januari Winters, aren't you? The one who looks after her sisters."

"Yes, I am..." I verified.

"And... you're friends with Amycus Derby. I saw you with him in the park in Newgate."

"That's right," I said, wondering where this could be going. It wasn't unusual for people to recognise me in my home town, this was a fairly regular occurrence, but the mention of Amycus puzzled me.

"Well, could you give him a message from me? My name's Sylvia."

"Okay..."

"Great. Well, tell him... that I'm sorry for everything, and that I was wrong to do what I did because it was the worst mistake of my life. I can't even begin to say how much I regret what happened. I still miss him, every day."

"Wow... okay, got it, but... what happened with you two?"

"Well... I knew him when we were in high school. I made a really stupid mistake, a wrong decision. What I did was unforgiveable. I'm a terrible person. He deserves better, anyway."

"Hmmm... I know what that feels like."

"What? But... everyone says you're such a good person. Jan Winters, the one who gave up everything for her family. You haven't done anything to hurt Derby, have you? Because if you have... I strongly advise you not to make the same mistakes I did."

"Well... I lied to him about my name and age, to get a job. I don't want to hurt him. He told me, all people have ever done was deceive him, pretend to be his friend then stab him in the back and... I'm not different. I'm lying to him too."

She flinched.

"What is it?" I asked.

"I was one of those people. Who pretended to be his friend, then stabbed him in the back. I left him to bleed as well. I didn't realise how bad a thing I'd done to such a good person until after I lost him. He's forgiving, but I don't think he'd ever trust me again, not after what I did. I bloody broke his heart. Stupid."

"Do you mean... you loved him?"

"I did, and letting go of that is pretty damn difficult, but... one bad decision wrecked my entire life. Try to put things right now, Januari Winters, while you still can. Otherwise, you'll lose him like I did, and if you can't see what a great guy he is, you must be blind."

"No. Actually, I... well, he's one of the best people I've ever met, and that is saying something."

"Well... just don't make the same mistakes I did, Januari. Don't break his heart."

"Oh, no. It isn't... we're just friends. He'd never think about me like that. I'm not that lucky. I have to go, I'll be late for work. Bye, Sylvia."

"Bye, Januari. Remember to tell him what I said."

"I will. Bye," and then I went to work.

I taught a Year 8 Citanian class first. It made me think of my own Year 8 sister. Things had improved dramatically since I'd been in to talk to her Head of Year. She was friends with Mary and Raul, the immigrants from Citania. She was telling me about the time she spent with them every day. I was so glad things were finally sorting themselves out.

The first thing I talked to Amycus about was Sylvia.

"Amycus, I was talking to someone earlier. She wanted me to tell you something, from her. Her name is Sylvia."

He froze, "*what?!* Sylvia? Are you sure? Blonde hair, glasses, quite tall, has a habit of tucking her hair behind her ear when she's nervous?"

"Yeah, that's her. I would listen to what she had to say if I were you."

"Okay."

"She said to tell you that... she's sorry for everything. She was wrong to do what she did, because it was the worst mistake of her life. She also said that she can't even begin to say how much she regrets what happened, and she still misses you every day. Those were her exact words."

"No..." he shook his head, not quite looking me in the eye, "she's just playing with my emotions. She can't have meant that. It was never real, we were never even friends. She said so herself. I've moved on, anyway. There are other people."

"It sounded like she meant it to me. It sounded like she really loved you. She said that what she did was unforgiveable, that one bad decision had ruined her life, and that she didn't realise she loved you until after she lost you."

"She didn't lose me. She pushed me away. She kissed Jake Barker, and then I came in and saw her. She doesn't love me, Janet; no one ever has and I doubt anyone ever will. It's just you; you're so determined to see the best in everyone. I can't ever trust Sylvia Edwards again."

"That's what she was afraid of. She seems really nice to me, but it seems like yours wasn't the only heart that was broken."

"I don't want to think about her. I want to forget I ever knew she existed. Please, Jan, just leave it."

"Okay."

"You know, after what happened with her, I swore not to trust anyone with a pretty face, because beauty seems to be used as nothing more than a weapon nowadays."

"Well, if you go by that rule, trusting me must be easy."

"Actually... it is now because I know you but at first... that is the precise reason I kept telling myself you weren't to be trusted."

I laughed, "Amycus! You're wrong about that, you know. You're just saying it to make me feel good about myself."

"No, I mean it. Anyway... you know yesterday you told me your dreams? What is it that you actually expect from your future?"

"Well... I used to think that my life was completely planned out for me already. It was going to be quite frankly boring, but recently, things have taken an unexpected twist, and... I don't think things are going to happen like I thought.

I'm not sure if that's a good thing or not. I have absolutely no idea what's going to happen to me next. I've never felt so... helpless, like I've lost control of my own life. I don't know what to do."

"Don't worry, Janet. I'm sure it will all work out. You're strong. You'll get through it."

"You're right. I have to, and I have to keep telling that to myself."

"I never really knew where my life would take me. All I ever really wanted was for my dream to come true, but I know now that it won't.

I'll probably just end up being a teacher at Newgate for the rest of my life, but I'm happy the way I am, really. With you as my friend... I couldn't really want anything more."

"Well, I'm glad you don't have anything to worry about. When I was little, I used to be so... innocent, with not a care in the world. Completely carefree. I've changed so much. I'm still the same person, but... my life has changed dramatically, and you know what? I'm glad.

If my situation had been different, if I hadn't had to... do certain things, I wouldn't be the same person. I'm glad things are the way they are. My life might be hard, but... I'm used to it."

"The way you cope with things is really remarkable, Janet. Inspirational, really. I wish I was brave like you. Whatever it is you're finding hard, you'll get through it. You just need to have courage. Keep constantly reminding yourself that you've got everything under control, and it will get easier. You have the strength to get through this."

It was so easy relating to Amycus; it just came naturally. Now we were talking like friends, because that was what we were, and it made it easier to think of him as only a friend.

It just made me feel guiltier for lying to him. It brought that regret back to the surface, all that regret for what I'd done, the feeling that I'd made a mess out of my life. There always seemed to be something to worry about at the moment. I needed to be wary, yes, but I needed to relax as well.

"Thank you, Amycus. You always seem to know exactly what to say to me."

When I got home that evening, I decided to spend some time with my sisters, because it would help to put my mind at rest.

We played a game of Unixudi, in six teams of two. I went with December, Februari with November, March and Octoba, April and September, May and Augusta, and June and July.

We ordered takeaway pizza and chips for tea. We had a really nice evening, and it did make me feel better. Then we had a movie night, all squashed up on the settee with December on my lap, and November on Februari's lap. We could just about all fit. It was a big settee. I didn't know what we'd do when December and November were bigger.

After all the others apart from Februari had gone to bed, Februari and I watched a film by ourselves. It was nice spending time with Februari. It was also quite rare. I was so busy nowadays.

After she'd gone to bed, I sat and read my book until I'd finished it. When I went to sleep that night, my mind was blissfully clear. I spent a while standing at the window, gazing up at the night sky. It really was beautiful.

I decided to go for a night-time walk before I went to bed. I took my usual route. I felt the pleasantly cool night air soft on my skin. I felt the grass, still wet from the last rainfall tickling my ankles where my trousers and socks were both too small.

I saw the moon glowing palely. The stars scattered across the sky around it. I remembered an ancient Larenian myth, in which one of the gods had knocked over a jar of pure light, and it had scattered everywhere and created the night sky. I'd used to be extremely interested in ancient Larenian mythology. I didn't remember much of it now.

As my mind wandered, I remembered that traditionally, names could only end in I, A or O. A for a girl, O for a boy and I for gender-neutral, but when people had travelled to other places, we picked up habits from other cultures.

That night, when I got back, my thoughts returned to my everyday life. I wrote my letter again as I did every evening.

Dear Father,

Things are getting easier. Today it was easier to just be Amycus' friend, but I still love him, underneath, and I'm not sure what to do about it. It's so easy to relate to him, and I feel like he understands. When I talk to him about anything, he always knows exactly what to say to me.

This evening, I spent some quality time with my sisters. We played Unixudi; and we had a movie night. Then I watched another film with Februari; then I finished my book and went for a night walk. It really helped to clear my mind.

I think I'm getting used to it, and I'm a lot more optimistic about this whole scenario. It won't be long before I have everything back under control.

It won't be long before everything is sorted out, and I'm so glad. Before I know it, I'll be well on my way to developing a normal routine again, so I can proudly say, 'Everything is under control.'

Love, Januari

Chapter 20

Jag önskar...

I wish... - Swedish

The following morning, May was crying. I went over to her, concerned. May almost never cried. There must be a serious problem.

I went over to talk to her, "May? What is it? Are you-?"

"Don't you dare ask me if I'm all right," she snapped.

"May, you can talk to me."

"No. You can talk to me. Why is it that you look after us? Does Mum not care about us? Did we do something wrong? Why do you do it, Januari? Why don't you go off and travel the world like you wanted to? Why do we never see you any more? Why do you have no time for us? Why are you always in such a rush nowadays?"

"I look after us because Mum is depressed. You know how much she loves Father."

"A lot more than she loves us, clearly," she scoffed.

"No, don't say that. She loves us. She just finds things hard."

"Just go away, Januari. I don't want to talk to you. You're just as much of a child as the rest of us. You're just a teenager."

"May, I know how you must be feeling. I know things are hard."

"No. You shouldn't be able to tell us what to do. You're only a child, like us. Why can't we have a normal life, anyway? Everyone else has holidays, and parties, and presents, and days out. I want to be normal. All I get is a mum who doesn't care about me and a sister who likes to play the grown-up, and now you're shutting us out. You don't care about us either, do you?"

"I got a job, May. I did it for you, because I love you. I want you to be able to have a normal life, as much as possible. I want to spend time with you. I didn't realise you were so upset about this. Don't worry, it's only natural. Why don't we talk a bit, and..."

"I said, I don't want to talk to you. You need to stop playing the grown-up, Januari. I want a normal life and a sister who can look after us properly. Ooh, that hurts, doesn't it?"

"You know what? I don't know why I bother," I shouted, "I don't know why it had to be me, I should be somewhere else right now, but instead I'm stuck here. I could have gone off to college with my friends, but I didn't. I stayed. For you. Now all I'm getting out of it is you yelling at me that I'm not enough, because no one ever asks how I feel about all this, and maybe it's hard for me too. Maybe I feel like I'm falling apart at the moment with everything that's going on in my life. I gave up everything for you, and this is how you repay me."

"You see? You know you aren't enough."

"I'm trying my best, all right?"

"Well, your best isn't good enough! You've let us down. You failed," she screamed. I froze, silent. I wanted to think she didn't mean it. I wanted to think she was happy, and that all of my sisters were coping fine, but this was May, and I believed every word she said.

"I'm going to school," she said finally, picking up her bag and coat, and ran out of the door. I didn't try to stop her. I just stood there, rendered speechless by her harsh words. What I'd said to her – I regretted it immediately. Just when I thought things were getting better.

I took my sisters to school and nursery. I didn't even notice anyone talking to me. I tried to act normally. I taught my lessons. I couldn't really think about what had happened until lunchtime.

I didn't want to talk to anyone. So I went into the corner of the language office, and put my head in my hands. I didn't cry. I just tried to hold myself together. At one point, Brian came over and asked what was wrong. I told him I was fine, and just needed to think, so then he went away again.

Later, Amycus came in. He went over and sat down next to me.

"Hello, Jan. I... are you all right?"

"I'm not the one who matters," I said, and then I burst into tears.

"Janet!" he stared at me, astonished. He'd probably realised that I wasn't as brave as he thought I was.

"Oh, Jan. Why don't you come to my classroom with me? If you want to talk about it, you can talk to me. Or we could talk about something completely different to take your mind off it. Or you could just sit and read your book. Either way, we won't be disturbed. No one ever comes near my classroom. Beware, the dragon lurking in La6."

I laughed shakily. I stood up in silence, and followed him. When we got to his classroom, we sat down.

"So, Jan... what do you want to do?"

"I think telling you would make me feel better." He nodded, and then sat there patiently while I let everything out, "the thing is, my sister May... she's usually really cheerful, but this morning, she got really, really upset, and she shouted at me. I tried to be understanding, but she wouldn't listen to me.

She said that... that I shouldn't be able to tell her what to do, and that I wasn't looking after her properly. That I didn't care about any of my sisters, that I was just someone unimportant playing the grown-up. I said I was doing my best, and she said that it wasn't enough, and I'd failed. The thing is... she was right. About everything. I am a bad person, she was just the first to see it.

I don't know what to do, Amycus, I feel so alone. I always try to do the right thing, but I always make a mess of everything. I can't get anything right. There's so much going on in my life at the moment, and I'm falling apart. I don't know if I can do it any more. I just can't.

I just want them to be happy, I've given up everything for them, and they clearly aren't happy. I don't know what to do. This is all driving me insane.

No one else has ever been in my situation; no one understands. No one ever bothers to think how I feel about things. Everyone expects so much of me, and I try to be positive. I'm trying to be everything for them, but I'm... not. She's right, I have failed.

I feel like you understand because you always know what to do, but there's so much you don't know. I feel as if when you find out the truth, you'll realise that I'm a bad person, and you won't want to be my friend any more. I wouldn't blame you. I just... I'm on my own, and I don't want to be. Oh, Amycus, I'm just so stupid, I can't do anything right."

He looked at me, speechless.

"I'm sorry, Amycus."

He leaned across and put his arms around me. I hugged him tightly.

"Oh, Jan," he said sympathetically, "I had no idea. I'm so sorry, I wish there was something I could do. I'm sure she didn't mean it. She was probably just having an off day, and was taking it out on the people closest to her. You aren't a bad person. I'm sure everything will work out."

He was so reassuring. I sat in silence for a couple of minutes, with my arms around my friend, and then my phone rang. I let go of him suddenly. I kept my phone on while I was at work in case either of the schools or the nursery needed to call me. My sisters were my priority. I picked up the phone and answered it.

"Hello, this is Jan."

"Hi, Januari. This is Annabelle, the school nurse at Oldgate High School."

"Hi, Annabelle. Yes, I remember. What is it? Are my sisters all right?"

"Well... May seems to be quite unhappy. She's in a terrible state. She's been crying uncontrollably for most of the morning. She's in no fit state to learn."

I froze, "May?"

"Yes. She keeps saying she doesn't think you'll forgive her. Did something happen?"

"She was upset this morning, I'm not sure what triggered it. She wouldn't talk to me."

"Well, she won't talk to anyone now, and if she won't talk to you, I don't know what to do. She's not well at all."

"Oh, poor May. The thing is, I'm at work at the moment. What should I do?"

"Well... if she could just be with you, she'd feel a lot better, I think. Would you be allowed to bring her to your work with you?"

"I'll check. I think I can make it work. I'll be right there. Would you tell May that... Jannie loves her no matter what, and that I'm on my way, and that I'll always put my sisters first."

"Okay. Thanks, Januari. I'll see you soon."

"Yep. Bye."

I hung up, and looked at Amycus.

"Let me guess – your sister May is ill and you have to rush off immediately to go and get her and bring her here, you're sorry you have to go, thank you, goodbye?" he asked. I laughed.

"Yes, exactly. I really am sorry, Amycus. Thank you so much. You always know exactly what to do."

He smiled, "why don't I come with you? I can drive you there if you like."

"It's fine. You've done enough for me already today."

"I don't mind. You don't want to make your sister walk too far, do you?"

He had me there. "Okay. Thank you, Amycus."

So he drove me to Oldgate High School, after I verified with Brian that it would be all right to bring May to Newgate. He said it would be fine as long as she didn't disturb anyone. When we got there, and I saw May waiting in reception, I called out to her, "May!"

She looked up, "Jannie!" She ran straight into my arms and I held her tight. "Jannie, I'm so sorry. I didn't mean any of that. I had a nightmare where you ran away from home and left us. I don't know what happened. I'm so, so sorry."

"It's okay, May. I will never, ever leave you. I love you, and I always will. No matter what happens. Let's go, yes?"

"I love you too, Jannie. Yes, let's go."

She took my hand and we left. I thanked Annabelle before we went. On the way back to Newgate, I realised something.

"I have a free period last, so I can take May home then. I don't know what I'm going to do for Period 4. I have a Year 10 Citanian class."

"I have an idea. I have a free period next. May could always come into my classroom, and I could keep an eye on her for you," suggested Amycus.

"Amycus, you don't have to-"

"Do you have another idea? I just want to make things easier for you."

"No. Okay then. Thank you," I turned to May, "May, this is my friend Mr Derby. You're going to go with him for a bit, in his classroom while I teach a lesson. Is that okay?"

"Yes, that's fine. Hello, Mr Derby."

May was acting a lot more like her old self now. I was so glad. So that was what happened. As soon as my lesson was finished, I went to find Amycus and May.

I knocked, and entered the room. May sat reading a story in a notebook, one that March had written called 'A Tragic Tale.' Amycus looked up, and smiled when he saw me.

"Thank you, Amycus. For everything. I'll see you tomorrow."

He walked over to me, "I'll see you tomorrow, Jan. Just remember, you *can* talk to me."

"I know. Talking to you always makes me feel better. I don't know what I'd do without you."

He smiled, and I smiled back. Then I went over to May.

"All right, May-May, come on. Let's get you home."

"Yep. Thanks, Mr Derby."

As soon as we were off the school premises, she nudged me, giggling, "ooh, someone fancies Mr Derby."

"May! Shhhh! What makes you think that?"

"Oh, come on," she scoffed, "you kept smiling at him, and, seriously; 'talking to you always makes me feel better, I don't know what I'd do without you.' Is that something you say to your friends?"

"May. Really. He's just a friend. He doesn't even know my real name. It isn't like that."

"You can't fool me, Januari Winters. I've never seen you act like that before. Have you told Febs?"

"May, there is nothing going on between Mr Derby and myself. He's my good friend, that's all."

"Yeah, yeah. Whatever you say, but I think he likes you too. Did you see how when you walked into the room, he sat up straighter, and smiled, and his eyes sort of lit up? Oh, and the way he looked at you – like you were the most precious thing in all the world."

"You're wrong. Amycus would never think about me like that, and I can't think about him like that."

When I got home, I wrote my letter immediately.

Dear Father,

This morning, May got really upset and shouted at me. The things she said were really painful, she might as well have stabbed me with the sharp knife in the kitchen. She says she didn't mean it.

I'm worried about her because it makes me think she isn't happy. All I want is for her to be happy, and all the others too.

I was upset at work, but Amycus looked after me. It makes me realise – I don't think I have it in me to stop feeling this way about him. He's just so... he's everything I dreamed my true love would be like - but it isn't like that, and it never will be. He always knows what to do and what to say to make me feel better. I just can't keep myself away from him, and what's inside my heart, it scares me.

Love, Januari

When I went to bed, I found a note under my pillow, in May's handwriting. It was as follows:

Dear Jannie,

I think you should tell Amycus Derby that you like him. I think you should stop refusing to admit to yourself how you really feel, and to us. You might not be able to see it, but I can. You should at least say something to Febs. It isn't every day that you find someone like that, and I really do think he likes you too. Honestly, he was looking at you like you were the most beautiful thing he'd ever seen. Sweet dreams.

Love, May

I didn't know what to say to that. May was probably just trying to make up for what she'd said that morning. I smiled, and put it in the drawer with my letters to Father. Then I lay down, and was asleep as soon as my head hit the pillow.

Chapter 21
จะอยู่คนเดียว
To be alone – Thai

I didn't mention May's letter or the subject it concerned to anyone the next day. It was a nice, normal day, much as it had been two days previously.

March, however, pulled me to one side before I left.

"Jan, I need to talk to you," she told me, "May told me that you have a friend at work, a Larenian teacher."

"May needs to know when to keep her mouth shut, and yes, his name is Amycus Derby. I think you'd get on well. What about him?"

"She said you were in love with him. Is that true?"

"Oh, not you as well! Okay, maybe I am, but don't tell her I said that." I went slightly pink.

"I won't. I'm not stupid, but I want to know – do you plan on telling him? Or Febs, or anyone?"

"I can't tell him. He wouldn't think about me like that, and I'd just lose his friendship, but what I do plan on telling him is the truth about myself. He deserves to know. I will tell Februari... tomorrow morning."

"Okay... and just so you know..." she hesitated for a moment, "from what May says, I think you and him are perfect for each other. A Larenian teacher, looked after you when you were upset... he sounds really nice. I'd like to meet him. Februari met him last week, didn't she? Can I talk to her about it?"

"Yes, but tell May not to tell anyone else, and don't tell Febs that I told you."

"I won't. I mean, I will. I mean, I'll do exactly as you said. Sorry. Also... don't be afraid to admit your feelings to the people who love you and, more importantly, yourself. Have a nice day, Jannie. I love you."

"I love you, too, March. You have a good day."

I was glad I had March for a sister. She was very intelligent, and shared my passion for reading. She also loved writing stories.

Later that day, I was talking to Amycus, as usual.

"Yesterday, Jan, you said you felt alone," he was saying, "I can't help but wonder why that is."

"The thing is, I'm pretty much living in two different worlds. My world at home, and my world at work. I'm finding it so hard, because nothing is constant.

When I'm at home, I have my sisters, and when I'm at work, I have you, but the reality is that I'm switching in between the two, and in that I am alone. There's something I'm not telling my sisters at home, a secret, but there are also things I'm not telling you, here. My sisters don't know what my work life is like, and you don't know what things are like for me at home. Like I said, nothing's constant. So in my reality, I am alone."

"I wish there was something I could do, but I do understand, at least to some extent. You see, when I'm at home, I really am alone. No family, no anyone. I'm stuck with the reminder that I am forever alone."

"You aren't."

"What?"

"You aren't alone any more; you have me. I'm your friend. I'm here for you, and you can talk to me about anything. I'll always be your friend, even if you aren't always mine."

"I'll always be your friend."

"I'm thinking that I'm going to tell you my secret soon, if you want. You'll never see me in the same way again. Really, I'm not who you think I am. My name isn't Janet Woods. The person you know me as is Janet Woods, and I'm afraid you won't want to be friends with the real me."

"Oh, I think I will. I'm not going to let the only friend I ever had slip through my fingers that easily." He grinned, "you said the other day that your sister November was saying that you would get a happy ending, and that she must have you mistaken for a fairytale princess. I have to say, it's an easy mistake to make."

He took my hand and kissed it, "oh, most beautiful Lady Janet, it is an honour to make thy acquaintance."

I laughed, "the honour is all mine, oh, kind Sir Amycus."

"Wouldst thou care to accompany me on a leisurely stroll in the park?"

"That would give me great pleasure, good sir." We both laughed, and then stood up and went for a walk in the park.

We went past a patch of roses. Amycus paused to pick one.

"That which they call a rose, by any other name would smell as sweet," he quoted, smiling. He held out the rose and I took it.

"Honestly, Jan. I mean it. I don't care if you have a different name. The person I'm with now, that's you, isn't it?"

"Yes, of course."

"Then it doesn't matter to me. The person I know as Janet Woods might go by a different name, but that doesn't make you a different person. You're still you. You're my friend, this person I'm talking to right now. Trust me, Jan."

"Amycus, my real name is-"

I was interrupted by the bell ringing back at Newgate.

"Come on, let's go back now. You can tell me another time. Don't worry about it."

I found that I was ready to tell him the truth, and at the right time, I would tell him.

After work, I was just leaving when Amycus caught up with me again. "Janet!" he called, "have you got a minute?"

"Not really, I have to get home, and there's loads of other things I need to do when I get there... I'm sorry, I meant: Yes, of course. Why?"

"Well... there's something I wanted to show you. Come with me. It won't take long, I promise."

"Okay," we went to the woods in between Oldgate and Newgate - the Silver Woods - and down by the river.

He jumped across to the other side of the river without a second thought, so I followed him across.

There was a cave on the other side. I'd been in this cave before, but hadn't noticed the small antechamber at the side. The entrance to it was very small, but we could both get through.

What I saw amazed me. I took a sharp intake of breath. The small cavern itself was beautiful, with part of the River Wild running through it, and spiral rock formations. All the walls were covered in chalk drawings of people and beautiful scenery. The drawings were very simplistic, yet so beautiful.

The rock in Lilidell was a special kind that was only found in Larenia, and when people drew on it, the drawings stayed there forever – it was one of the only magical things that existed in Lilidell, because we couldn't be completely separate from the rest of the country.

"Amycus..." I whispered. I simply stood there, stunned into silence as he began to recount memories of his past.

"I used to come here a lot as a child. I always brought candles for the light and the warmth, and so that I could see to draw. I found that no one ever disturbed me here. It was easier to imagine myself away into another world, with nothing but the dark walls and the sound of running water.

The drawings on the walls were of my imaginary world – I called it Amarevia. I had friends there, Trystan and Emma. I always wished they were real. It hurt me that they were just made-up characters in a made-up magical realm, but... I used to have adventures there, and there were people that cared about me, people who understood... it was everything to me.

I'll tell you something, Janet, I still like to imagine I'm there sometimes. I still like to come here, and make up more stories. I used to write them down in my notebook, but... then Jake took it and showed everyone, so I burnt it."

He stared at the walls, seeming to be a million miles away. This cave was filled with echoes of a young boy who felt alone, who grew up alone and made up a fantasy world to live in. It was something really special. Who was I to be seeing all of this?

"Why are you showing me all of this? It seems like something you'd want to keep private. It's amazing. Why me?"

"It is true, I've never shown this to anyone before, but I wanted to show you, because... you're my friend. My only friend, and that means all the world to me, Janet. You're like a real life Emma."

I was so touched by all of this that I decided to try and tell him how I felt about him.

"Amycus, I need to tell you something. Besides my secret. I... you mean a lot to me." *That wasn't what I was supposed to say.* I thought to myself. *That isn't the same thing.* "I don't deserve you as a friend, and I don't deserve to be seeing this. I don't know what makes me different from anybody else."

"What makes you different is that you're kind, brave, intelligent, beautiful and selfless. You don't judge people, and you have helped me to find myself again. You're one in a million, Janet Woods."

"No, I'm not any of the things you said, Amycus. I'm just... an everyday girl who needs to get her priorities straight, trying to find her way. You treat me like I'm something special, but I'm not. Everyone has friends. Yours just happens to be an average girl who lied to you about her identity, and who's fallen in love with the wrong person," I stopped suddenly, realising what I'd said. Someday, I was going to go way too far.

Amycus looked at me, speechless. Then he spoke, "Janet..."

I burst into tears of sheer frustration, "I'm sorry, Amycus, I'm so sorry. I never meant for any of this to happen, and I want to tell you the truth, but I don't know how. I need you to carry on being my friend, but I don't deserve to have you as a friend. I... oh, I'm sorry. Don't worry, I'm okay." He seemed slightly bewildered.

"Oh, Jan. I'll always be your friend. I trust you, you don't have to be afraid of telling me the truth, and... I understand exactly what it's like to fall in love with the wrong person."

"Oh. I... what's she like, the person you're in love with? Besides lucky, of course."

"She's... the sweetest girl I've ever met. She was there for me when no one else was. She's stunningly beautiful, and more importantly is kind and always tries her best, and is modest and selfless. She's the one person I can be myself around, and she reminds me a lot of myself."

"Well, it sounds to me as if she's perfect for you," I said wistfully, "you should tell her how you feel."

He shook his head, "I can't find the words, but how about you? What did the person you love do to deserve that?"

"Well... he's very intelligent, and kind, and I don't know what I'd do without him. There's no one else like him. I could talk to him forever and never get bored. He makes me smile, a real smile. He's always patient with me, and he looks after me when I'm upset.

I haven't known him long, but... I don't know what I'd do without him. He has a lovely smile, and it reaches his eyes, and the way he looks at me... he's always so gentle, always the gentleman. He would never think about me like that. Besides, he's in love with someone else."

"Well, the girl I love is in love with someone else as well. I suppose that's just the way things are."

"Yes... I wish things were different, but they aren't. Anyway... I really need to go now. I have to get home, and my sisters will be waiting for me. Thank you for showing me this, it means a lot. I'll see you tomorrow, Amycus," I stood up to leave.

"Janet, wait."

"What?"

"I... never mind. I'll see you tomorrow, Jan."

"See you tomorrow."

On the way back home, to my astonishment, Sylvia – that woman who Amycus had known long ago and who spoke to me the other day – ran up to me, "Januari!" I was nearly home when she came up to me, and I had almost all of my sisters with me.

"Sylvia. What is it?"

"Trust me, Jan, this is very important. You said that you'd lied to Derby about your name and age. Did you tell him your name was Janet Woods?"

"I... how do you know that?" Nothing made sense to me about this conversation.

"Yes! I knew it! Right, now listen to me, Januari; this is more important than you know. You have to tell him the truth about yourself, and soon, I can't keep this up for very long."

"What?" this was getting more confusing by the minute. I didn't understand why she kept coming up to me like this. What was she trying to accomplish?

"Just trust me on this one, okay? You love him, don't you? Well, you've got to tell him the truth, Jan. Do it for him. You have to tell him you love him."

"Are you out of your mind? Then I'd just lose his friendship. Amycus would never think about me like that."

"Oh, yes, he would, and... he does, Januari. He loves you, and once he knows the truth about you, there won't be anything holding him back from being open with you about how he feels. He isn't the kind of boy – sorry, man, I forget that we aren't kids any more – who makes the first move, so you have to tell him how you feel. I know it will be hard, but trust me, it's worth it to be with him. If Amycus Derby thinks about you like that, then you're the luckiest girl in the world. He needs to know, and to hear you say you love him too. That would mean everything to him. It'll be worth everything, I promise. Just please, listen to me."

I looked at her, astonished, "no, Sylvia, you're wrong. He doesn't love me. We're just friends. I can't tell him how I feel about him, I can't. I will tell him my real identity, and then... we'll carry on being friends. I need to go now, goodbye."

"Januari, wait. There's more. I have to tell you – for him to hear you saying the words, 'I love you,' would mean everything to him. He's never had anyone say that to him before, and he needs to hear it. You two were made for each other."

"You're wrong. Amycus deserves better. Goodbye, Sylvia," I said firmly, and then I walked away with my sisters.

"What was that about, Jannie?" asked July, "it sounded like something out of a romance film."

"Bleargh," put in June.

"Oh, nothing. It was just about my friend at work," I said. Then I walked in silence until we got home.

When I got back, I put the rose he'd given me in a glass of water on my bedside table, and I wrote my letter.

Dear Father,

I had such a lovely day today. I went for a walk in the park with Amycus. I told him that my name wasn't really Janet Woods. So he picked a rose and gave it to me, saying 'that which they call a rose, by any other name would smell as sweet.' He says he doesn't care what my name is as long as I'm still the same person.

I was just about to tell him my real name when the bell rang to go and teach our next lesson. I'm not afraid of telling him the truth. I am ready to tell him the truth.

I love him, and I know I can trust him. Tomorrow, I will tell Februari that I love him. I'm not going to keep secrets any more. I don't know what I'm going to do about the fact that I'm in love with him, but I will certainly accept it now instead of trying to stop it.

I don't think I can tell him that, but I'll see what Febs thinks it's best for me to do. I know she'll probably give good advice, but it looks like things are getting easier.

Love, Januari

Chapter 22

Tôi không thể đủ khả năng để làm điều này

I cannot afford to do this - Vietnamese

The next day, I sat on my bed looking at the rose and thinking about Amycus. I knew I could trust him, but part of me still didn't want to.

I was still afraid of falling in love. Everything could go wrong. Februari came and sat next to me, and looked at me.

"Jan, are you all right?"

"I don't know what to do, Febs! I think I'm falling in love," I burst out.

She stared at me, "*what?!* Who? This isn't like you, Januari."

"I think I'm falling in love with Amycus Derby."

"Ah... I thought so. The way you were acting around him last week... I did wonder."

"What should I do?"

"I think you should tell him."

"I can't, Febs. He would never feel that way about me. We're just friends."

"You might be surprised."

"That's extremely unlikely."

"If you really think so. We can talk later, when there's more time. You need to go now or you'll be late for work."

"Okay. I'll see you later, Februari. I love you."

"I love you too, Jan. Think about telling him. Just think about it."

I went on my way, determinedly not thinking about it. I talked to November instead, suggesting games she could play with her dolls.

On the way to Oldgate Junior and Infant School, I talked to June. A girl in her class, called Alicia, had introduced her to rock music, and I recommended some good bands.

When I was walking to work from the nursery, I tried to think about other things as well.

I was teaching Ella Wright's class just before lunch. She came up to me after class and whispered "Enjoy your last afternoon here, #@*%£. I'm telling Mr Marsden after school today."

I couldn't think about anything else for the rest of the day. I was so scared. At lunchtime, I was telling Amycus about Jemima, Victoria and Genevieve, but I couldn't concentrate on what I was saying. I just about managed to act normally, but inside my head I was absolutely terrified. I wanted to tell Amycus the truth then, but I couldn't bring myself to. I knew that was probably the last time I'd ever see him.

"Janet," he said, and I jolted out of my thoughts, "Jan, is everything all right?"

"I hope so, Amycus. I hope so."

When I said goodbye to him, I hugged him tightly, knowing that I was saying farewell forever. It took everything I had not to burst out crying.

That afternoon, I had my favourite Year 9 class. The first class I'd ever taught. I saw that they had Amycus next for Larenian. So while they were getting on with some silent work, I wrote a letter to him.

Amycus,

This is the hardest thing I've ever had to do, but I'm going to have to resign. One of the students – Ella Wright – knows my secret, and she's kept quiet for this whole term. She doesn't know for certain because I didn't let on, but she believes she's right. I know she plans to expose me after school today, so it won't be long before everyone knows my secret.

If you still want to hear it from me, I would gladly trust you, but you should know that I am a liar and a deceiver, and I don't deserve your friendship or your forgiveness. All I'm going to say now is that I am not who you think I am.

I wanted to apologise for lots of things, but above all, I'm sorry it had to end this way. I'm sorry I wasn't able to say goodbye to you properly.

I wanted to write this letter to thank you for everything you've done for me, and to say goodbye. I know you'll probably never want to see me again.

So I suppose this is goodbye. Forever. I'll miss you. I will think of you with every passing moment. There is nothing I regret more than this. Farewell, Amycus.

Love, Januari

(Janet Woods)

I also wrote another bit on the back. A postscript. I didn't know if he'd see it, but I wrote it anyway, just in case.

There is also something else that I admit I should have told you – I love you. I love you, Amycus Derby, because you're the best person I have ever met; you were always there for me just at the right moments when I needed you. I know you won't feel the same, but you deserve to know. Leaving you is the worst moment of my life. Please don't hate me, and I hope that one day, you'll find it in your kind heart to forgive me. I am truly sorry. For everything.

After the lesson, I asked Mia Casey to stay behind a minute. She was the one student that I knew I could trust not to read it, and to give it to Amycus.

"Mia, would you do something for me?"

"Yes, of course."

"I saw on the register that you have Mr Derby for Larenian next. Would you give him this letter? Tell him that it would be best to wait until he is alone to read it, and that I'm sorry."

"I will, and I'll make sure no one else reads it but him. I'll see you next lesson, Miss Woods."

"Goodbye, Mia. Thank you. You're one of my best students, you know that? I really enjoy teaching you."

I would miss Mia when I left. She truly was a wonderful student, and I knew that she would go far in life.

At the end of the day, I went into the language office to get my things. I shivered. I saw Ella Wright already in there. I heard her telling Brian the truth about me. There was nothing I could do.

"Well, I had been thinking she looked very young for a 21-year-old. Janet? Is this true?"

"I... I'm sorry, I never meant any harm, I-"

I was interrupted suddenly by the door opening, and Amycus came in. My heart leapt at the sight of him. I hadn't thought I'd ever see him again.

"Brian, don't believe a word that student says about Janet. She was just trying to get her fired, making up stories like that," he burst out.

I took a sharp intake of breath. Now he was lying for me, to try and keep my secret. He knew I'd lied to him, and he was still helping me.

"You know I'm right, Mr Marsden. Look at her. Does she look like a 21-year-old to you? You can see, she's uneasy because her secret's finally out," Ella accused.

"Who are you going to believe, Brian? Your work colleague or a student?" argued Amycus.

"I believe you both. I think that she really is the person Ella says she is, but I also believe that Ella was trying to get her fired. Ella, that will mean detention, you realise."

Ella scowled. Amycus looked at me anxiously. I gave him a strained smile. Ella turned and exited the room before anyone could utter another syllable.

"Brian, it wasn't because I wanted to. I had my reasons for doing this, but I'll go now. I want you to know that Newgate is a fantastic school, and the students – with a few exceptions – are really lovely. I hope they benefit," I put in.

"Brian, please let her keep her job," begged Amycus, "she had good reasons for doing what she did. She's a good teacher, and it was a whole lot of hassle getting a teacher in the first place; you don't want all that again, do you?"

"You're right," Brian replied, "She is an outstanding teacher. Frankly, I'm surprised at how well she does her job, being so young. Finding a teacher is a lot of hassle," he looked at me, "you can keep your job, Januari. Just keep up the good work. Now, I suggest you get yourself home. I'll see you on Monday."

"Thank you," was all I could say. I stood up, and headed out of the door. Amycus caught up with me just outside the building.

"Januari," he called. I halted, and waited for a minute. He came over to me. "Why don't you let me drive you home? It's been a long day."

"Okay," I said softly, "Amycus, I-"

"It's all right," he reassured me, "you don't need to worry."

"When I get home, if you want you can come back inside with me. I want to tell you the truth. The whole truth."

"Okay."

I called home and asked Februari to pick up November and December for me, and then we slowly wandered back to his car in silence and he drove me home.

Chapter 23

Mna nzulu akazange abone ukuba lowo uzayo

I seriously did not see that one coming – Xhosa

I welcomed Amycus into my house, and immediately, I was surrounded by my sisters.

Februari, holding December, wanting to talk to me about what we'd been discussing earlier. March, wanting to show me her latest book. April and May, wanting to tell me about their days. June, wanting to tell me about the music she'd been listening to. July, wanting to give me a bracelet she'd made. Augusta, wanting to show me her latest artwork. September and Octoba, wanting to tell me about a game they'd devised. November, trying to get to me through the forest of legs.

"Okay, okay," I picked up November, and took December from Februari.

"Februari, April, May, June, I promise I'll talk to you later. March, I can't wait to read your book. I'm sure it's amazing. July, that bracelet is lovely. I'm so lucky to have sisters like you. Augusta, that picture is absolutely incredible. Jemima would be proud of you. *I'm* proud of you.

September, Octoba, I can't wait to hear all about your game. November, I promise I'll play with you soon. December should be going to sleep. Just a minute," I sang my lullaby to December quietly, to lull her to sleep.

"Let me take her for you. I'll make sure she stays asleep," said Februari immediately, taking December from me, "you go upstairs with your friend, Jan. I'll put on a film or something, and you come down when you're ready."

"Okay. The first one into the living room gets to choose the film," they all scurried off.

"Thank you, Febs. I don't know what I'd do without you. I love you."

"I love you too, Januari. Now go."

I led Amycus upstairs, into my bedroom (which was the only place I could talk to him in private). I closed the curtains, and we sat on the window sill seat.

"Now, I'm sorry about all that. Are you ready for me to tell you the truth?"

"Of course. You can tell me anything, and by the way... you have a beautiful singing voice."

"Thank you. I made up that lullaby for my sisters when I was little. It's silly, really, but... it does help them get to sleep."

"Is there anything you can't do?" he asked, and I laughed.

"Okay... My name is Januari Snow Winters, and I am 17 years old. My mum is called Summer and my father is called Jack. I have 11 sisters, all named after the months of the year.

When I was nine, my father was diagnosed with lung cancer. When I was ten, he was taken into hospital, and only allowed monthly visits home. That was when Mum started suffering from depression, and I had to look after my sisters. So when everyone else couldn't or wouldn't do anything, it fell upon me, as the eldest sister, to step up and take charge.

So I've looked after my sisters since I was ten. I'm nothing special, just an ordinary girl. I gave up my possibility of a happy ending in exchange for my sisters' happiness. All I want is for them to be happy, and I wanted to get a job so that they could live a better life. A more ordinary life. I try so hard to be everything people expect me to be.

So there you have it. That's the real me. Januari Winters, and I wouldn't have got this far without you."

"...Thank you for trusting me with the truth."

"I would trust you with anything, but... Amycus, I want you to tell me something."

"Anything."

"Last week, someone saved your life. You talked a bit, and you told her about me. You said-"

"Hold on, how do you know about that?"

"Same reason she knew so much about us. It was me."

"*You?* Jan... you saved my life."

"Well, it's what any decent person should have done."

"How can I ever repay you?"

"By answering me this one question: Did you really mean what you said that night?"

He reached out and took my hand, "course I did."

"You said you would forgive me. Do you?"

"How can I hold it against you, when you did it for your family who you love? *Of course* I forgive you, and what is forgiven can then be forgotten."

"Then you have more than repaid me. In fact, you've given me so much that I owe you."

"No, you've given me everything," he shook his head, his gaze distant, "when you hugged me, it was the happiest moment of my life."

"Well, there has to be more to life than that. How are you going to top it?"

He laughed, "I think I have a vague idea... Close your eyes." It was a request, not a demand.

"Why?"

"Just trust me."

"Sometimes you are a mystery to me, Amycus Derby," I closed my eyes, smiling. He took both of my hands, and then he spoke.

"You make me unspeakably happy and only you. I've never had anyone before. No friends, no family. At the orphanage, they called me 'Friendless.' It wasn't creative or original, but it was true, and that hurt.

I used to dream that one day, someone would care. That I'd live happily ever after, that I'd have someone there for me, that I wouldn't have to be alone any more...

You really are quite angelic in my eyes. Like a fairytale princess. All I want, all I care about, all I've ever dreamed about, all I've ever wanted is you, my Januari."

And then he kissed me. *Kissed* me, just once, and after a moment's surprised hesitation, before I could stop myself, I kissed him back. That moment, that single moment, was the happiest moment of my entire life.

He smiled, "I think I may have a new happiest moment of my life."

"I love you," I told him, "so much." The words fell so naturally from my mouth, because it was the first time I'd had the courage to say them.

"No. That's not possible. No one would think about me like that. That isn't how it works. I thought you were in love with someone else. I don't get *you*, I don't deserve that."

"Amycus Derby. I promise you, I do love you with all my heart. I was talking about you yesterday, it was always you. I don't even deserve your friendship, let alone anything more. I'd do anything for you. It's always been that I'd do anything for the ones I love. Anyway, what happened to the person you were in love with?"

"Januari, isn't it obvious? I was talking about you."

"*What?!* But you said... stunningly beautiful? I thought... Sylvia."

"You are, in my eyes, and no, Sylvia gained my trust and then left me alone. You have never hurt me, and I trust that you never will."

I shook my head, "I love you. Believe me, I love you."

He surveyed me thoughtfully, "what do you see in me, Januari?"

How could I explain the reasons behind my feelings for him? I loved him because he'd been so kind to me, and because he understood me. He was completely unique; he was intelligent, and he made me smile. He was everything I'd ever dreamed my true love would be. I decided to at least attempt to explain.

"I've been so, so lucky, Amycus. I entered willingly into pretty much a whole different world, and immediately you were there by my side. You showed me around and helped me; you talked to me when I needed someone to talk to, and spent time with me so I wasn't alone.

You were my best friend, I fell completely in love with you, and didn't tell you, and when I revealed what a bad person I was, that I'd *lied* to you, an innocent man, your response was to *kiss* me. That's lucky."

"To the contrary," he replied, "I've been as lucky as it gets. Since I was a very young child, I've dreamed of true love, of romance. I had no family and no friends. All I ever got from other people was hatred and cruelty.

When I was about 12, I lost hope completely. I sank as low as it gets – I was alone, I was miserable and depressed, and I closed my eyes to the fact that not all people were bad. My heart grew cold. I grew up alone and hopeless, and I got a job. I worked well, I have done for two years now.

Then you came, and I was different. I was genuinely interested in what you had to say, hanging on your every word, making an effort. Through you, I found myself again. I became a better person, and I smiled for the first time in over a decade.

Then you trusted me with the truth about yourself. When I found the courage to try to show you exactly how much you meant to me, you told me that *you loved me*. Me! The miserable young man who people only looked at out of pity.

I was so sure you only treated me like a friend because you felt sorry for me, and I still can scarcely believe it. You are the everything to my nothing, and the shine to my sun; without you, my world is a dark, lifeless place. You brought about something from nothing, Januari, and... you are an amazing person, even if you don't see it. I love you so, Januari Winters."

That was the first time I'd actually heard him say that. It made my heart beat faster than ever before. Before I knew what I was doing, my lips were on his and I was kissing him again. He hesitated for a second, and then he kissed me back. He put his arms around me, pulling me closer. It was like I'd completely lost control of myself.

"Now what did I do to deserve that?" he asked, smiling.

"You said you loved me. I... you... oh, Amycus."

"Yes. I'll say it again: I love you, Januari. You are everything to me."

"I love you, Amycus. More than I can say."

I put my arms around him, and hugged him tightly, overwhelmed with emotion. This was the best thing that had ever happened to me. I'd fallen in love, and then I discovered that he loved me too. Maybe it was possible for me to get a happy ending after all.

However, I didn't know what I was going to do with myself after that. I was only going to see him at work. This just made the fact that I couldn't have a happy ending more obvious.

"Amycus... why me? There's nothing I can give you. I'm just an ordinary girl. I'll only see you at work. You deserve someone who can spend time with you, and..."

He shook his head, "no, Januari. You were never ordinary. You're hardworking, and determined, and beautiful, and brave, and strong, and... well, we'll just have to treasure the time we can spend together, won't we?"

"There are lots of other girls, who could spend more time with you, and who could give you so much more than I can. You know Sylvia still loves you."

"I don't want Sylvia. I want you. I can't have it any other way. Is that so hard to believe?"

"Actually, yes."

"Oh, Januari. Well, if it's any consolation, I feel the same way. I don't understand why someone like you would love someone like me."

"Well, if you want proof, look at that letter I wrote you. On the back."

"There was more?"

"Yes."

He found the letter, and read out:

"'There is also something else that I admit I should have told you – I love you. I love you, Amycus Derby, because you're the best person I have ever met, you were always there for me just at the right moments when I needed you. I know you won't feel the same, but you deserve to know.

Leaving you is the worst moment of my life. Please don't hate me, and I hope that one day, you'll find it in your kind heart to forgive me. I am truly sorry. For everything,'" he sighed, "Januari... did you really mean all of that?"

I smiled, and put my head on one side, "what do you think?"

“It’s best not to ask that question.”

“Of course I meant it, Amycus! Of course I did. I had to tell you because I thought I’d never see you again. It would have broken my heart to leave you. I want you to know that, and remember... I love you. That won’t ever change.”

“I love you too, Jan, and I always will.”

“...We’re going to have to go now. I have to get back to my sisters; they’ll be wondering where I am.”

“Okay.”

So I went back down to my sisters, who were watching a film, supervised by Februari. I turned to Amycus, “I’ll see you on Monday, Amycus. I love you.”

“I love you too, Januari. I’ll see you on Monday.” After he left, I went and sat with my sisters. I was in a very good mood for the rest of the day. I made us tea, and I played with September, Octoba and November. I made sure I did everything my sisters wanted me to do.

Chapter 24

רופן נאָענט

Close call – Yiddish

That evening, I went out to do the shopping. I thought that if I could get it done, then maybe I'd be able to do something nice with my sisters at the weekend.

I found that I didn't need to write my letter that night. I didn't need to confide in a piece of paper, when I had Amycus. I could tell him anything now. I trusted him completely. Whatever happened, I could talk to him.

I felt as if I'd had an immense burden lifted from my shoulders. I didn't have to keep secrets from anyone any more.

I started crossing the road, and was halfway across when I saw another car screeching around the corner, with a woman in the driver's seat, looking petrified. I heard the brakes screaming, and then all of a sudden, I felt light, and dizzy. Then everything went black.

I opened my eyes. I felt disorientated. Where was I? I sat up, and looked around. Everything was white, or light green-blue. A hospital. I was in a hospital bed.

A doctor with short blonde hair and blue eyes came over to me.

"Hello, Januari. My name is Dr. Marsden. I believe you know my husband, Brian, through work."

"Yes... it's nice to meet you, Dr. Marsden. I... what happened?"

"Well, there was a car crash. The driver of the car had a heart attack, we don't think she'll survive the day. Don't worry, there's nothing you could have done. You haven't broken any bones, but you're going to have some quite nasty scars. You've been unconscious for one night."

"Oh. What happened to my sisters? I need to go home, to look after them. I feel fine now, really. Thank you."

"Whoa, not so fast. You're Jack and Summer Winters' eldest daughter, aren't you? Your parents want you to go and see them. Your father seems to have taken a turn for the worse."

"Oh... okay. Hang on... Mum's here? What about my sisters? She can't just leave them by themselves."

"I wouldn't worry about that. Oh, and I almost forgot – Mr Derby was here. He found you first, after you got hurt. He called the ambulance, and then he came here with you, and he stayed until we wouldn't let him stay any more. I expect he'll be here again soon, to see you."

I smiled. Dear Amycus. That was so like him – and my heart ached to see him, but my family had to be my priority. I went off to find Father, without another word.

When I was nearly there, Brian caught up with me, "Januari. Fancy seeing you here! Oh, of course – my wife Melody told me a little about you. You must be here visiting your father. I've been meaning to talk to you. I was just here to talk to my wife, she's a doctor here, but could I have a word with you now?"

"Okay."

"Mr Derby – I know he's your friend, but... don't expect too much from him."

"What's that supposed to mean?"

"Well, if you happened to be... in love with him, I would advise you, he doesn't think about people like that. You'd be wasting your time."

"Okay. Thank you. Goodbye, Brian," I walked away from him, and entered the ward where Father was.

I hurried over to him.

"Father! I'm here."

"Hello, Jannie. I heard you were in a car crash – are you all right?"

"I'm fine. Father, how are you?"

"Not very well, I'm afraid. I fear I haven't got long left here."

"No. No, you can't die."

"You're strong, Januari. You'll cope. I'm very proud of you. I wanted to talk to you about-"

"Januari!" called a familiar voice. I turned around, and there was Amycus. Without a moment's hesitation, I started running towards him. He ran over to me, and threw his arms around me. He held me close, and I hugged him tightly. "My Amycus," I whispered.

"Dear goodness, you had me scared. I've been so worried about you. Are you all right?" he said all at once.

"I'm fine. It would take more than that to injure me badly. Dr. Marsden told me you stayed with me until they wouldn't let you stay any more."

"Of course I did. I didn't want to leave you. I didn't want you to be alone," he replied softly.

I went over to my parents, and said to them, "I'll be back in a minute. I just want to talk to my friend here." They nodded, and Amycus and I went out of the room. I turned to him.

"Um... Brian was talking to me earlier."

"Uh oh. What did he say?"

"He said not to expect too much from you, and that if I was in love with you, to remember that you don't think about people like that."

"Ouch. He has *no idea.* He sees the man on the outside and thinks that's all there is. Everyone thinks that. Except you – you didn't judge me. You got to know me, to really know me, the man inside... the gentle, loving one.

I was lost, cold and alone, down a path in a cave as old as time. Many have gone down that path and never returned. Most people take one look at that path, and... and give in to their fear. They avoid it, but you went down that path and took a lamp with you.

You found what was lost. You showed me the way back. You showed me the way back, so that we could continue down a new path together.

When you found me, you shone the light on my face and I was dazzled, after not seeing light for so long. All the way back down the dark path, I thought it was the fire in your lamp dazzling me. Even now, on the new path, I am still dazzled, even though there is light everywhere.

When we got back to the light, I realised that it wasn't the light dazzling me – it was you. I love you,

Januari Winters, and don't let anyone tell you otherwise."

I was rendered temporarily speechless. I was really touched that he'd said this. "I love you too," I replied, "I was never going to listen to him, anyway, and... thank you."

I kissed him, pulling him close to me. I imagined what it would have been like if things had been the other way round. If he'd been injured. I knew exactly how he must have been feeling.

There were no people around, so he put his arms around me, and held me close. I didn't want to let him go, but we had to go back to my parents.

He grinned, "I could definitely get used to this."

I laughed, "All right, all right. Come on, let's go back into the ward. Oh, and Amycus... you'd better get used to it."

He raised his eyebrows. "Are you flirting with me?" he teased.

I elbowed him playfully, "you started it!"

He laughed, "yes, I suppose I did. Sorry, couldn't resist."

I giggled, "come on, then."

So I turned, to go back into the hospital ward. I thought about what had happened. I remembered the car, and the driver. So I went to go and find Dr. Marsden, and ask what had happened. Amycus came with me.

"Dr. Marsden, what happened to the driver of the car? Was she all right?"

"Why don't you go and see her? She wants to apologise to you."

So I went to find the driver of the car. She sat up straight when she saw me. "Miss! I am so sorry. I apparently had a heart attack. Are you all right?"

"I'm fine. How about you?"

"Well... the doctor said that... my heart could go wrong again at any time and I probably wouldn't survive a second attack. I have so much I regret. My daughter never forgave me for... and my son. I never saw my son. I was trying to find him, for Liza."

"I'm sorry to hear that. My name's Januari Winters."

"I'm Susan Derby."

"Susan Derby? You had a son, who you never saw?"

"Yes. His name was-"

"Amycus."

"Yes. How did you know that?"

I froze. Amycus was standing at the other side of the room, talking to Dr. Marsden. "Amycus!" I called. "Come over here a minute." He came over immediately.

"What is it?"

"Hang on..." said Susan Derby. "What did you just call him?" Amycus looked at her.

"My name is Amycus Derby," he said uncertainly.

"*Amycus Derby?*"

"Yes. Why?"

"Then it's you. You're... my son," she said faintly.

He stared at her. "What? But... I don't understand. I thought..."

Then the doors opened, and a young woman came in. Her hair was exactly the same colour as Amycus', and she had the same grey eyes. She came over. "Mum, what's going on? You said... I got here as fast as I could."

"Liza," said her mother, "I think... I think this is your brother."

"What? Amycus?"

"Hang on a minute, can someone please explain to me, what's going on here?" interrupted Amycus.

"My name is Liza Derby," said the woman – Liza, "and I once had a twin brother, called Amycus but Mum abandoned him when we were babies. I never knew him, and she never told me about him. Then, I found a picture, and I found out. So I ran away from home, and tracked down my Dad. I've been living with him, and searching for my brother, since I was ten.

Are you really my brother? Because if you are, I want to apologise for what Mum did. She tried to make excuses, but really, it's only because she... she loved our Dad, and then he left her, when he found out about us, and she blamed you, which was wrong, but I've been searching and searching, and Dad too.

Dad's gone now; he just disappeared last year. They found him dead a week later, but I carried on looking for my brother. Prove it, what's your middle name?"

"My middle name is Charles," he answered, slightly bewildered.

"Yes! Then it is you! I'm your twin sister." She threw her arms around him. I saw him freeze awkwardly.

"I'm sorry," she muttered. "I just... I've been looking for you for so long. I realise... I'm a stranger, really, but I hope you'll let me into your life, and I hope you'll forgive me."

"Of course. It wasn't your fault. It would be nice to get to know you. I'm just not used to having a family."

"My son, I'm so sorry. I was wrong. There is no making excuses for what I did. I see now... what a lovely young man you've grown up to be. It was the worst mistake I ever made, giving you up. Forgive me, Amycus," said his mother.

"I forgive you," he verified. His face was impossible to read. His hand found mine. "Januari," he whispered, "I really... I'm not very good with people."

"Don't worry. Just be yourself. I appreciate this must be very overwhelming. I should probably go now anyway. It will be easier for you to be alone with your family," I whispered back.

"No, it's easier when you're here. You're more my family than they are, Jan," he murmured.

I was touched by this, as I knew exactly how much it meant to him. That he considered me more his family than his own mother and sister.

"Amycus, my father... I need to be with *my* family."

"Is everything all right?" His voice was full of concern, and he'd stopped whispering.

"My father... isn't going to be here much longer."

"Oh, Jan. I'm so sorry. I'll come with you. Unless you'd rather I didn't."

"No, I want you with me, but you need to stay with your family." He exchanged mobile numbers with his sister, and came with me. I needed to find my father before it was too late.

Chapter 25
Idagbere, Baba
Farewell, Father – Yoruba

I went over to my father. Amycus was with me. "Mum, Father," I began tentatively, "I want to introduce you to-"

"Let me guess," sighed Father. "Amycus Derby?"

I frowned. "How do you know that?"

"Well," he pulled out a stack of paper from the locker beside his bed, "your mother found these in your room. They were addressed to me, so... she brought them here for me to read."

I saw then that they were my letters. "Oh no. I never meant for anyone to read those. Father... you didn't read them all, did you? No one was supposed to see those."

"That much was evident, and yes, I did read them all. I'm sorry; I was curious, but I have to admit, you did sort of leave me hanging. It was like a story in which my daughter is the main character, and then you just stopped right on a cliff-hanger."

"That's because I had no need for confiding my deepest secrets in a piece of paper any more. I have Amycus."

"What are those, Jan?" asked Amycus, "now I'm curious."

I laughed. "Those, Amycus, are letters I never meant to send. Like a diary, of part of my time at work. I needed to talk to someone, but I didn't feel like I could."

"You can trust *me.*"

"I know I can. Which is why..." I paused, and took my letters from Father. "...I'm giving them to you to read." I held them out, and he took them uncertainly.

"Are you sure? If these are really where you confided your deepest thoughts and feelings, are you really sure you want to share them with me?"

"Of course I am. I trust you, and you can trust me. When you've read those, you really will know everything about me. I don't want to keep anything from you."

"Thank you. It means a lot that you'd trust me with that."

"I would trust you with anything." He smiled gratefully.

"So, Jan, are you going to tell me what happened yesterday? Did you tell him?" Father asked pointedly.

"I told him the truth, yes."

"And what about... the other thing that you were worried about?"

"What do you mean?"

"Don't try playing dumb. I know you were trying to ignore it, but I promise you that isn't the way to do it. Did you talk to Februari?"

"Oh! Oh, that. Yes, I did tell Februari, and I told Amycus too."

"Told me what?" put in Amycus. I turned to face him.

"I love you," I said softly. He sighed.

"What did you say to that, Mr Derby?" asked Father.

"Please, call me Amycus, and... actually, she only told me she loved me after... I kissed her."

"I'm sorry, you did *what*?!" choked Mum.

"I kissed her. I wish I could say I was sorry, but... I'm not. Your daughter Januari is the most incredible person I've ever met. She's determined, and intelligent, and independent, and brave. She perseveres endlessly for what she believes in, and I couldn't help but fall in love with her. I hope you know how lovely your daughter is."

Father beamed at me, "I won't say 'I told you so,' because I didn't, but... I had a hunch things wouldn't happen like you expected." Then he started coughing, and the coughing fit went on for a good few minutes. "I'm sorry." He smiled sadly.

"Now, my sweetheart..." He turned his gaze to Mum. "Soon, I will be going somewhere you can't follow."

"I have to, Jack," she said, her voice thick with tears, "I can't lose you. I need to be with you."

"Summer, you are needed here. We will meet again, in the next life, but for now, my love, we have to say goodbye. Now, before I go, I want you all to promise me something." We all nodded, and he continued.

"Summer, I want you to promise me you'll stay here. I'm going somewhere you can't follow. Stay here. For me. For our daughters. Look after our daughters, so that Januari can live her life, and live your life yourself. Be strong. I will always love you, and I will be right with you, in your heart."

"I promise. I do love you, Jack," she sobbed.

"Amycus, I won't make you promise me anything, but please, take good care of Januari. When I'm gone, help her get through it. She needs you."

"I will promise. I will always stand by Januari. I'm sorry I couldn't get to know you better."

"And Januari. I want you to promise me you'll look after your sisters, and your mother. Your family needs you, but I also want you to promise me that you will live your life. Don't spend all your time with your family, but make sure you look after them. Oh, and..." he beckoned. I leaned in close, and he whispered into my ear: "never let go of your true love. It is the most precious thing in all the world."

"I promise, Father. I love you. I'll miss you."

"And I you, my darling. I'll be in your heart. One of my only regrets is that I never lived to see what a wonderful young woman you'll be when you grow up, and all my other daughters too... tell them I love them, and my Summer... I love you."

Those were the last words he ever spoke. After that, he lay back on his pillow, and moved no more. I dropped down onto my knees, sobbing, beside his bed. "Farewell, Father," I said, my voice full of emotion. I felt Amycus' hand on my shoulder, comforting me, but words failed me. I couldn't believe he was really gone. He'd been suffering for so long, but this had all been so sudden.

I was vaguely aware of someone saying my name in the distance. "Oh," was all I could manage to say.

"It's all right, Jannie. I'll go and tell them to leave you alone," said Amycus gently.

"Amycus... don't leave me. I can't... I need you."

"Don't worry, my Januari, I'll be back in just a minute." He went over to the people and talked to them for a minute, then came back.

"I'm sorry, Jan, they said that if you need to be with your family, I shouldn't be with you. If you can talk to me, you can talk to them. I tried reasoning with them, but they wouldn't listen. It's Brian and his wife."

"They don't understand."

"I know they don't, Jannie, they really aren't being fair with you. I'll just have to leave you with your mum. I'm sorry. I should have tried harder."

I took a deep breath. "No, it isn't your fault. Don't blame yourself. You did your best. I just... I'll miss Father, but life goes on, and I get left behind. That always happens to me. I'll talk to them. I just need you to stay with me."

"I won't leave your side, I promise," he assured me. I stood up, and he put his arm around me, and we went over to Dr. Marsden.

"Hello again, Januari. I'm sorry about your father. The thing is, we are happy to discharge you but going home probably isn't a good idea since you have your sisters to care for. You were actually very lucky but you still need complete rest."

"Januari," Brian cut in, "I have to apologise for what I said earlier. I didn't realise that you'd been a patient here. If I'd known... I would, perhaps, have acted more tactfully."

"Don't worry about it," I replied. I doubted he'd have acted with more tact, but it was nice of him to apologise. Brian was the sort of person that couldn't be tactful if he tried; the fact that he was talking to me now was proof of this.

"So," Dr. Marsden continued pointedly, "you need rest, and not many people around. Do you have any ideas?"

"I have to go home, my sisters need me. They'll be fine, honestly."

"Januari, you can't honestly say that the little ones won't come wanting to play with you, and the older ones won't want to talk to you, and the others will just leave you alone. From what your father said about you, you would get up to do whatever needed doing as well. You can't be getting up to do things, you need to stay somewhere else."

"She could stay with me," suggested Amycus. "In my spare room, and I'd make sure she was looked after properly. There are no other people."

"That's a brilliant idea, Mr Derby. Are you sure you can do that?"

"Of course."

"Januari? Does that sound okay to you?"

"Yes... if Amycus is sure, and if I really can't go back to my sisters."

"It will only be for one night. Then you can go home. I'll tell your mother where you are. It was nice meeting you, Januari."

"Likewise, Dr. Marsden."

Amycus kissed my forehead gently and, ignoring Brian's expression, we left in silence. I returned with Amycus to his house.

Chapter 26

Weji aan furfurnayn

An unfriendly face - Somali

Amycus invited me in. His house was one of those houses with a big metal fire escape staircase going up the outside of it. Inside, it was simply furnished but it looked very comfortable.

We sat down together on the sofa. "What do you want to do, Januari?" he inquired.

"I don't know. Why don't we just talk? I like talking to you. You always have something interesting to say."

"Okay. Why don't you tell me more about your sisters? What are they like?"

So I did. I told him about Februari first, then March, then April and so on and so on, but at one point, we were interrupted by a knock at the door.

"I'll be back in a minute, Januari." Amycus stood up, and went to answer it. Minutes passed. Then I heard someone sobbing, and a cruel voice teasing, and tormenting.

"Amycus?" I called.

"It's okay. Stay where you are," he called back to me, but I couldn't stay where I was, because his voice sounded shaky, like he was trying to speak normally when he was upset. So I went to find him.

He was kneeling on the floor, crying. I hated to see him like this. Amycus never cried. He was brave, so much more so than me. A man was standing over him. The man was tall, with blonde hair and blue eyes. I immediately recognised him as Jake Barker, the brother of the boy who'd broken my sister's heart. The man who, when drunk, had almost killed Amycus. All he'd ever done was hurt the people I loved.

I glared at him. "What are *you* doing here?"

"I'm sorry, have we met? I think I'd remember meeting someone like you."

"On a couple of occasions. One where your brother broke my sister's heart and one where you were drunk, and you almost killed the man I love."

"Well... I'm sorry?" He laughed.

"Januari," Amycus looked at me pleadingly, his eyes full of tears, "please, stay out of this. I don't want you to get hurt."

"No," I said simply. I held out a hand, and pulled him to his feet and said, "It's all right, Amycus." I turned my eyes to Jake. "I suggest you leave. You have no reason for being here."

"Well, the thing is, I don't feel like leaving just yet. You see, I'm curious. What are you doing here with Friendless?"

"Don't call him that. It isn't true. He has friends, like me for instance, and you know what friends do? They stand up for each other."

"Ooh, feisty," he grinned, "so, are you going to make me go?"

"If I have to."

He tried to knock me off my feet, but I dodged him, and the force he'd put in caused him to fall over. I smiled to myself. He was back on his feet in an instant.

"You see, girl, I'm not going to go away. You're going to have to make me, and that won't be easy." He looked at Amycus, and grinned, "I pity you, Friendless. Too much of a coward to stand up for yourself, letting her do all the standing up for you. I bet this is your only friend. I didn't think you had it in you to actually make friends with someone. Now you're still exactly like you were; you haven't changed. You're still nothing. Nothing at all – you're pathetic."

"How dare you speak to him like that?!" I burst out, "do you have any respect for him at all? No one is nothing, and if you speak to people like that, you'll be the one who's friendless."

He laughed, "I'm sorry, you have the wrong person. Everyone wants to be my friend."

"I have no idea why," I responded coldly.

Jake turned to Amycus again, "so, Friendless, who is this? Your girlfriend? So, you've forgotten what happened with Sylvia already, have you? Oh, sorry, were you hoping I wouldn't bring that up? You see, I never thought you'd move on from Sylvia. Especially with your ideas about true love."

Oh, so now Sylvia had come up again. I wondered what really happened between them, I had a feeling Amycus had been keeping it from me. Amycus looked away. "Jake," he said, "I know you did that just to hurt me, but... Sylvia was never my friend, let alone anything more. She never even cared about me at all. I... haven't forgotten, but you know she broke my heart. It was your fault."

"Yeah, everyone prefers me to you, Friendless."

Then I had an idea, and I wondered if it would work. Jake seemed to be the kind of person who relied on other people paying attention to him. So if Amycus and I had some sort of drama which didn't involve him, maybe he'd go away.

I threw my arms around Amycus. "Don't listen to him, Amycus," I said out loud. Then I whispered to him, "pretend you don't love me. Just pretend."

"Why?" he whispered back.

"Jake relies on other people paying attention to him, and enjoys making people suffer. If he thinks we're suffering without him there, and we're just ignoring him, I think he'll go away. It might be the only way."

"...Okay, but I don't like it."

"Me neither. All right, now don't stop for anyone, not even me, until he's gone. Now push me away. Go on."

"I won't mean anything I say. For this, I am truly sorry," he whispered mournfully, and then he pushed me away.

"No," he said, "no, this isn't right."

"What do you mean?" I looked at him, appalled.

"What I mean is that you're right. You are no different to anyone else. You're exactly the same. You lied to me."

"I don't understand. You said you forgave me. You said you loved me."

"I thought I did, but really, I was lying to myself. The person I thought I loved was Janet Woods, and then I discovered that she doesn't exist. Instead there is a 17-year-old playing the grown-up and wearing the face of someone who was my friend."

"This is me, this is the real me."

"I don't want the real you. How do I know I can trust you?"

"I'm sorry," I reached for his hand but he snatched it away.

"It's too late for that," he said abruptly, "I was never meant to spend time with people. I have to learn to live alone."

"You don't have to be alone."

"I want to be. All people are the same. Cruel. Liars. Full of hatred. The one person I thought was different was lying to me all along. I'd rather be alone."

"I love you."

"Then you're wasting your time. I never want to see you again, and you," he turned to Jake, "you have some nerve coming here, after all you've done to me. Get out."

"With pleasure," said Jake, "I'll leave you two to... argue. Good luck, girl." He went out of the door.

Amycus locked the door, and then promptly collapsed against it.

"That was the hardest thing I've ever had to do. You *genius,* Januari Winters."

"We did it. You're a very good actor."

"You, too. I can't believe we really did it. I love you, Januari."

"I love you too." I leaned up to kiss him, and then he touched his lips to mine, and put his arms around me, holding me close. Then he frowned. "Jake. At the window."

"Who cares about him?" I answered.

"Fair point," he wiped his eyes, "thank you for everything back there. I just... thank you."

"It's okay. Are you all right?"

"I am now you're here."

"Anyway... can you tell me more about what happened between you and Sylvia?"

"I... she was my girlfriend once. I knew her all through high school, and we started going out in year 10 and then... I saw her kissing Jake, and she told me that it was never real. She was never even my friend. That's why I found it so hard trusting people as time went on. I was afraid they'd just deceive me like Sylvia did for 5 years... she broke my heart. I thought she cared about me, but she never did."

"Oh, Amycus. So... why did you trust me? That must have been hard."

"I couldn't exactly help it. There was just... something about you that struck me as different to other people, and... it turns out I made the right choice in trusting you, didn't I? You're not like Sylvia. You won't break my heart."

"I would rather die than break your heart. I love you, Amycus, and... I'm sorry about what happened with Sylvia."

"I'm sorry I didn't tell you before. I just... couldn't bring myself to. I couldn't help it. She treated me like I was something special, Januari, and then I found out that... it was never real, but... I should hope that you're real, now that we've got that identity problem out of the way."

I laughed, "I assure you, I am real, and I don't intend to hurt you, ever. You can trust me."

"And I do trust you, Jan. Can I talk to you about something else?"

"Of course."

Then we went back into his living room, and sat down.

"Januari," he said, "I want you to imagine you're in a valley, right at the bottom. There are lots of trees, and there's a river. Can you see it?"

"Very clearly."

"Good. That valley is in a place called Amarevia. It was my imaginary world when I was a child. Now we're both there, but we're not alone. There are two other people there as well, called Trystan and Emma..."

We continued like this for the rest of the day, making up things that were happening in Amarevia. It felt very real. He introduced me to Trystan and Emma, and then he showed me all around Amarevia, both of us imagining it vividly.

At the end of the day, he started reading my letters. I sat next to him, and that night I fell asleep in his arms.

Chapter 27
اندھیرے
Darkness Descends – Urdu

I opened my eyes, and immediately realised I was alone. I got up, and went to look for Amycus. The house was silent.

So when I'd looked in every room, I ascended the staircase, and found him on the roof. The sky was black, and rain was pouring down. Amycus stood, gazing out across the black sky.

"Amycus?"

"Ah. This complicates things slightly."

"What do you mean? I don't understand."

"I have to go."

"*What?!*"

"Januari, listen to me. I love you, but you don't love me. You think you do, but you're wrong about me."

"No, I do love you. Don't ever think otherwise. Don't do this."

"I have to, because one day, you'll find your true love."

"You are my true love. I couldn't ever love anyone but you, Amycus. You have to listen to me."

"When I'm gone, you'll realise. You don't love me, and you never have. You don't know anything about romantic love. You don't understand it."

"No, don't go, don't leave me. Please, I am begging you, Amycus; don't break my heart."

"I won't break your heart. I don't have your heart. One day, you'll find your true love, and you'll be glad. You'll forget me."

"No. Never. Please, please, I can't lose you. I love you. Believe me, Amycus, I love you."

"You don't, but I love you. Goodbye, Januari." And then he stepped off the edge. The rain lashed down, slicing us apart, ripping through the air between us and preventing me from getting to him. I was too late.

"Nooooooo!" I screamed, "Amycus!" I ran down the metal steps, and they echoed dully. He lay on the ground, unmoving. I ran over to him.

"No, Amycus, no, stay with me. Stay with me, I love you. Don't leave me."

"I'm sorry, but you weren't meant for me. You couldn't possibly have been meant for me. You're the most amazing person I've ever met, Januari Winters. I don't deserve to be with someone like you."

"Amycus, I'm just an ordinary girl. An ordinary girl who loves you. How could you do this to me, how could you take yourself away from me?"

"I'm sorry. I never meant to hurt you."

"You thought this wouldn't hurt me?" I was shivering, and my hands were going numb with cold. I looked at him, tears springing to my eyes as I tried to comprehend why he would do this.

"I thought you were asleep. I know now I've made a huge mistake. Oh, what have I done?"

"It'll be all right. You can do this. Just hold on, hold my hand."

"I can't live through this, Januari."

"You can't go, you can't leave me. Amycus, I love you."

"I love you too. My Januari." And then his heart stopped. I held him tightly in my arms, and closed my eyes as if that could make it go away.

"Oh, Amycus, my Amycus," I wept.

"I'm here, Januari." I heard his voice clearly in my head. "It's okay. It was just a dream. You can wake up now. Open your eyes, Jannie."

"But I'm afraid of what I'll see."

"Don't be. Trust me. I'm here."

"Either this is really just a dream, or I'm talking to a voice in my head."

"It's all right. Open your eyes. I'm here. Be brave, Januari. You can do it."

"I love you, Amycus," I told him, and then I opened my eyes and there he was. I threw my arms around him. He held me close.

"There now. I've got you, Januari. It's all right," he said gently.

"I thought I lost you."

"It's okay. It was just a dream. It isn't real," he reassured me.

"It felt real."

"Do you want to tell me about it?"

"I... I don't know if I can."

"Okay, okay. I think I have a vague idea, anyway... you were talking in your sleep."

"Uh oh. How much did you hear?"

"All of it, I think. You... I left you?"

"Yes. You went where I couldn't follow, and you wouldn't listen when I said I love you. I was begging you to stay with me, but there was nothing I could do. You have to believe me, Amycus, I love you. I felt so helpless, and you wouldn't listen to me."

"Januari... you know I would never do that to you, don't you?"

"I don't know. Under some circumstances..."

"Jan, I have a reason to stay alive. As long as I have you, I want to stay with you. I know you love me, really. I believe you. I love you too."

"I know. I was so scared, though," I shuddered.

"You don't have to be afraid. I hate seeing you upset, because you're usually so brave."

I gave him a weak smile. "There. Now I'm not upset any more."

He smiled, "my brave, brave Januari."

"You say so much about me that isn't true, Amycus. I-" I paused, seeing the clock on the other side of the room. "Amycus. It's three in the morning."

"It is. What of it?"

"How long have you been right next to me here?"

"I... never mind that. If you must know, I was here the whole time. I never left your side."

"You stayed with me *all night?* You shouldn't have. Amycus, why did you?"

"Isn't it obvious? Because I love you, and you fell asleep in my arms. I didn't want to disturb you."

"What did I do to deserve you?" I asked weakly.

"I ask myself that question every day, and the answer is always 'I don't know.' But I suppose that's love, isn't it? The person you love most in the world will always seem perfect in your eyes."

"You're right. I love you, Amycus Derby."

"And I love you, Januari Winters."

He brushed a hair out of my face, and then I was gazing into his grey eyes, smiling. This was the smile that people had praised when I was a little girl. The one that only surfaced when I was feeling completely happy, right through to the heart. He leaned in and kissed me softly. I laughed.

"You always make me feel better, Amycus."

"Did I ever tell you how beautiful you are?" He said with a grin, and I laughed again.

"All right, enough of the compliments. It isn't true, anyway. I'm literally the most average-looking person there is."

"Not to me, and just because you don't believe something doesn't mean it isn't true. I would do anything for you; you know that, don't you?"

"I would do anything for you too. I wish there was some way I could make up for everything I've done. I lied to you, and you forgave me. It seems like I'm always having to thank you for things."

He smiled, shaking his head, "you don't have to thank me for anything. Everything I do, I do because I love you, and I can't live without you. You've done everything for me. You've saved my life, both metaphorically and literally. I owe you everything. Why don't you try to sleep some more? It's been a very rough day."

"Okay. Just promise me that you'll get some sleep as well. I love you."

"I promise. I love you too."

I fell asleep with those words echoing in my head. *I love you too.* For the first time, I completely believed that he did love me like I loved him. That was when I realised – maybe it was possible for me to get a happy ending after all.

Chapter 28

O que mais importa

What matters most – Portuguese

The next day was Sunday, and I was ready to go back home, feeling much better having rested after the accident. I was thrilled to see my sisters again. I went to find Mum, to see how she was coping.

"Mum? How are you?" I inquired, my voice sympathetic, but I could not have anticipated what she said next.

"You are not going to be hurt in the way that I've been hurt. I am your mother and for once I'm going to act like it. Young lady, you are going to resign from your job, and you are forbidden ever to see him again."

"*What?!* Why? Mum, don't do this to me. You're being ridiculous."

"No, I'm not. I don't want you to get your heart broken."

Amycus came over, looking disbelieving. "Mrs Winters, I would never break Januari's heart."

"Jack broke my heart, but he didn't mean to. He was taken from me. I lost him. I don't want my daughter to lose the one she loves."

"Please. I'm begging you. All I want is to make your daughter happy. She's all I have. I'd do anything for her. She's the most wonderful person I've ever met. Please..."

"Mum, please," I put in, "He's spent too long alone. He doesn't have anyone else."

When it became clear that this wasn't working, I decided to try something else.

"Mum," I started again, "do you regret meeting Father? Do you regret marrying him; do you regret all the time you spent with him?"

There was a moment's silence. Then she spoke again, "no. I don't regret the time I spent with Jack. He was my true love, but I lost him. My heart is broken. I can't risk the same thing happening to my daughter. I'll give you a minute to say goodbye, and then I want you to leave, Mr Derby." She went out of the room, leaving us alone.

"We'll work something out. I can't never see you again. I love you," I said immediately.

"No, you have to do as your mother says. She's just trying to take care of you. Now listen to me – even if we can't be together, I love you and I will always love you. I will never be able to love anyone else but you. I wish it didn't have to end this way."

"Oh, Amycus. It can't end this way. We have to be able to do something. I'm 17 years old. That's old enough to know what I want."

"Yes, I know, but you have to do what your mother says. She's in a delicate state. We don't have a choice. This has to be goodbye, Januari. Let's not make this any harder than it already is."

Then Mum came in, "All right, out."

I looked at Amycus, and he looked at me. I hugged him tightly. "Goodbye, Amycus. I love you. More than anything else in the world."

"I love you too, and I always will. I want you to promise me that you won't ever forget me."

"I'll never forget you. Don't ever forget – you're not alone, and that there is someone who loves you."

Mum pushed us apart. "That's enough. Leave."

"I love you, Amycus."

"I love you, Januari."

For a brief moment, our eyes met. I could see his were sparkling with tears. I grabbed his hand, and held it tightly, and then released it. I watched him leave, and then I burst into tears and ran upstairs. I didn't even attempt to hide my tears.

I couldn't believe my story was really going to end that way. If my life was a book, it would have ended at that moment, with the words *"She never saw him again. The end."* But my life wasn't a book, and my life continued.

I would think of him with every passing moment, think about how my story could have ended. The rest of my life was going to be a misery. The pain would pierce me like a thousand knives, and every living moment would be torture. At that moment I realised how much he really meant to me, how losing him was the worst possible thing that could happen to me.

Februari came over to me. "Jan? Can I give you some advice?"

"If you really want. I can't believe this is really happening."

"I know you're only 17, and that children have to do what their parents say, but you aren't an average 17-year-old. You're Januari Winters, and Januari Winters doesn't go down without a fight. Januari Winters never gives up, and besides, what would Father have wanted?"

"I did promise Father I'd never let my true love go... are you telling me to be rebellious?"

"Yep. Don't resign from your job. Go to him. Go now, and don't let anyone keep you from him."

I suddenly remembered something he'd said – *I can't live without you.* Now he thought he was never going to see me again. "I have to go. Right now."

"That's my sister. Good luck."

I grabbed my coat, and was straight out of the door, and it hit me – *I was going to see him again.* I was standing up for myself, and being rebellious. It felt great. I started running, running as fast as I could.

When I was about a quarter of the way there, a car pulled up beside me. I couldn't believe who was driving it.

It was an 18-year-old girl with short blonde hair and green eyes. Her hair had been straightened, since last time I saw her. She seemed very confident driving the car, though she clearly hadn't been driving long. She grinned at me.

"Hi, Jannie. Long time, no see. We've missed you."

"Victoria?" I gasped. "I thought you were in Rosamontis."

"Nope. We're back."

"We?"

"Yep. Jemima and Genevieve are in the back. We came because we needed to stop you from making a huge mistake. We got your letter, and you can't let your friend go."

A little while before this, I'd written a letter to my friends. I'd told them about my situation at work, and about Amycus, but I hadn't told them that I loved him. Now that was going to be hard to explain.

"Actually, that's why I'm on my way to see him now, because I won't let him go."

"Well, get in, and give us directions. We'll drive you."

So I got in the car and started giving them directions. "Oh, your timing is impeccable. Wow, I've missed you three," I told them, "how's college going?"

They all started talking at once.

"Great. I'm in the middle of doing a painting of our galaxy. I'm really pleased with it," I heard Jemima say.

"There are some foreign students studying Larenian. We met this nice girl from the Somnian Republic, called Ximena, and there's this guy from Mysteria..." Victoria explained.

"Victoria fancies Luciano, the guy from Mysteria," put in Genevieve, sniggering.

"Shut up, Genevieve! Well, I kind of do like Luciano... he's really hot. He has black hair, and he does it really cool, and he has these gorgeous grey eyes. I love guys with grey eyes, don't you? Grey eyes look like they're filled with mist, but there's light shining through it," Victoria babbled.

"Yes. I do love guys with grey eyes." *Well, at least, I loved a guy with grey eyes.*

"I am loving college physics. There's a really, really good view of the night sky from the room we're sharing. I wish you could see it, Januari," Genevieve informed me.

"Victoria, we're here," I said.

"Okay, we'll wait for you," replied Victoria.

"You three can come round to my house afterwards. I'll make us all something nice for tea."

They nodded. Then Jemima gasped, "Januari, look!"

A dark figure stood on the roof. It was pouring with rain, like in my dream. Then he stepped off the roof. I gasped.

"No," I whispered. Almost as if he'd heard me, he suddenly grabbed onto the roof with one hand, and he was hanging there, hanging on with only one hand.

"I'll be back in a minute, girls," I murmured. I got out of the car, and went sprinting over to the metal steps. There was a locked gate to stop strangers from going up there, but I climbed over it without a second thought and ran up the steps as fast as my legs would carry me.

I got over to him, and gazed down at him over the edge.

"Are you *insane?*" I called down to him.

"Probably," he replied, "what are you doing here?"

"I'm going to save your life again, whether you want me to or not. Hold on." Though I thought if he didn't want me to, he would have let go by now.

"I'm sorry," he called up to me, sounding as if he really meant it, "very sincerely sorry. I thought I would never see you again."

I ignored this, determined to get him to safety first. I held my hand out for him. "Take my hand. I'm not letting you go. This isn't the end. I will *never* even consider letting you go again."

He took my hand, and finding strength I never knew I had, I helped him climb back up onto the roof. "Are you all right?" I asked.

"Yes – thanks to you. You saved my life – again. Thank you."

"You had me scared, Amycus. Don't ever do that to me again." We were on the way back down the metal steps now.

"I won't. I promise, but how... I thought..."

"I love you. I'm not letting anything come between us."

"How did you get here so fast?"

"My friends are back from college. Just visiting, I think. Victoria drove me."

"That's good. Come back inside with me?" he offered.

"I can't," I said regretfully, "my friends are waiting."

"Later?" he persisted.

I considered. "Come round to my house. You can join us for tea. My friends will be there, but they won't mind. They'll want to meet you. They came back because they thought I was about to make the worst mistake of my life."

"And what was that?"

"Letting you go, and do you want to know what I promised Father, apart from that I'd look after my family? I promised him I'd never let my true love go. You, Amycus."

He smiled. By this point, we were back at the bottom of the steps. I turned to say goodbye to him. "I'll see you soon, Amycus. I love you."

He kissed me, and put his arms around me, holding me close. I hesitated for a second, feeling awkwardly aware that my friends were watching us, but then I couldn't resist kissing him back.

I couldn't believe I'd almost let him go. This man, that meant so much to me. That had done so much for me.

"I almost lost you," I said, and then I was kissing him again, frantically. I'd never really acted like this around him before, but I couldn't help it. I realised then, more than ever before, exactly how much I loved Amycus Derby.

I pulled him closer to me, not wanting to let him go, and one of his hands was in my hair, the other on my waist.

When, at last, we broke apart, he was the first to speak. "I love you, Januari Winters. Thank you again for saving my life."

"Anytime," I said, and he laughed, "I love you, Amycus Derby. More than I can explain." I gave him one last smile, and it was a really happy smile, the kind that only existed around him. Then I went over to Victoria's car, and got in, still smiling.

My friends gawped at me. Then, as usual, they all started talking at once. This time, I couldn't even distinguish who was saying what.

"Is that how you treat your friends nowadays, Jan?"

"Januari, you didn't tell us he was *that* kind of friend."

"Oh my gosh, Jannie, what the heck? Do mine eyes deceive me? Were you *kissing* that man?"

"Okay, slow down. I can explain," I said, laughing. We started driving, and I attempted to explain.

"What I didn't realise or was refusing to acknowledge when I wrote you that letter is that I am completely and utterly in love with him. You didn't know because, at that point, I didn't know myself.

On Friday, I told him who I really am. Then he told me that he loved me, and I love him too, so there you have it. I'm sorry I took you by surprise, but... I couldn't help it. I almost lost him. At least I know now, that won't happen again. So... yeah. That's it."

"Wow. Januari. I did not see that one coming. You got a boyfriend while we were at college and didn't tell us immediately?" Victoria said.

"Well, I'm not sure 'boyfriend' is the right word, exactly..." I pondered.

"Why? What would you say?" asked Genevieve.

"I'm not sure, actually. True love?" They all giggled. "What?" They laughed more, and I along with them.

"So, Victoria, tell me about this Mysteria guy? Was it Leonardo?"

"*Luciano!* And, oh, yes, he is without a doubt..."

"Oh, now you've really set her off. Well done, Januari," muttered Jemima.

Amycus came round that evening, along with my friends. Mum gasped when she saw Amycus.

"Mum," I murmured to her, "I'm old enough to make my own decisions. I won't allow you to take him away from me."

She sighed, "fine, if you really must. You've grown a lot while I've been shut up in my room."

Then I went over to Amycus, and took his hand. I led him into the dining room, and introduced him to my family and friends. My friends were pleased to meet him, but when he was introduced to March, some controversy arose between March and May.

"So, March," he said, "I believe you are the author of that story May was showing me, in the notebook."

"What? May! You weren't supposed to show it to anyone!" she moaned.

"It's good. Besides, I had a good reason for doing it."

"I'm really sorry, Mr Derby. No one was meant to read that yet. It wasn't ready," March apologised.

"Really? Because what I read was absolutely outstanding for someone your age. You are in Year 9, I believe?"

"Really? You liked it?"

"Very much. You're clearly a natural author."

"Thank you." Then she turned to May. "May-May, why did you show it to him?"

"I'll tell you later," replied May.

We all enjoyed the remainder of the evening very much, and then I bade farewell to Amycus and my friends.

I was glad to see that my friends were very much unchanged, and spending time with them came as naturally as ever it had. They'd told me that their plans were to stay in Oldgate overnight, and then go back to Rosamontis the following day. Which meant I wasn't going to see them again before they left.

"We'll visit more often, I promise," said Victoria. "Every weekend if we can. We've missed you too much."

"That would be really nice. I've missed you too. Give my regards to your friends Ximena and Luciano.

Victoria, don't get into too much trouble. Jemima, good luck with finishing your art project. Genevieve, enjoy the views from your room. Take care, all of you. It was really nice seeing you again. Goodbye."

"See you, Jan," Genevieve raised a hand in farewell.

"Bye, Jannie," Jemima grinned.

"Arrivederci, Januari," called Victoria.

I waved them off, and then turned to Amycus. I leaned up and kissed him briefly on the cheek. "See you later, sweetheart."

"Sweetheart?"

"Hmm... just trying it out. What do you think? No?"

He laughed, "your choice... darling."

I raised my eyebrows. "Just trying it out," he said, grinning, "what do you think? No?"

I elbowed him. "All right. Bye, Amycus. I love you."

"Bye, Januari. I love you too."

He smiled at me, and then he, too left. May came bouncing up to me. "I knew it! I knew you loved him!" she beamed.

"May. Don't go on about it, okay?"

"Yeah, yeah, whatever."

"Hey, Jannie," said April suddenly. "Mary and Raul introduced me to some really good music. Like, rock music. It's really cool."

"I'm glad you like it. It means you have good taste, and you didn't tell me Raul and Mary were into that kind of thing. We really have to invite them round sometime."

"Oh, yes, I'd love for you to meet them." She went skipping off upstairs. *Skipping!* I was glad to see April so happy. I smiled after her. I had raised my sisters well.

A few days later, it was Father's funeral. Amanda was going to be coming, to help comfort Mum. Amycus had said he'd come too. He'd been helping my family a lot since Father died, and I was extremely grateful for his help.

So we all went together. We'd organised that Mum and I would both say something about Father, so after she'd spoken, I got up to speak.

I stood at the front of the church, and tilted the microphone down so I could reach it. Then I started to talk.

"Well... it's been a long time since Father first fell ill. I can't believe it's all over. Father was a wonderful person, in so many ways. He always did so much in the community and when he was a vicar here, his services were memorable and he always went the extra mile.

He was such a good father to my sisters and me, and he always encouraged and supported us in whatever we did. Until he was ill, he was always there for me, and I always knew I could talk to him about anything.

I hope that people will see the same qualities in my sisters and me that could be seen in him, because he couldn't have set us a better example.

I know he'd want us to move on from this, and be happy. He always had such hope that things would work out well, and when he told me my dreams would all come true, I never believed him." Tears sprung to my eyes as I spoke. Amycus looked up at me and nodded encouragingly, so I took a deep breath and continued.

"I should have believed him, because my father was a great man, and he was right a lot of the time. It's hard to accept that he's really gone now, and some of my younger sisters won't even remember him. I'll never forget what he was like, and I'll always remind my sisters of what a wonderful person our father was.

I know that none of us here will forget Jack Winters, because he found a place in the hearts of everyone he met. It seemed like he was contagiously happy, and even when he was ill, he looked at it with a heart full of optimism, and hope, and love. Love was always important to him.

My father taught me so many important lessons, and I have always tried to live in his image because I can't think of a better person to be like. I know we'll find things hard with Father gone, but we'll try and do what he would do, and look on the situation with hope." I nodded, and then headed back down into the pew.

"Well done, Jannie," said September, smiling.

Amycus took my hand and squeezed it. "You did really well," he told me.

"Thank you," I smiled, and wiped my tears, "it'll all be okay."

I knew that it would. I had my family and Amycus, and my friends, and I didn't need anything more.

Part III

Unexpected ending

One year later

Chapter 29
ఆశ్చర్యం
Surprise – Telugu

A year later, I was still working at Newgate High School, and things hadn't changed a bit between Amycus and myself. The students now referred to me as Miss Winters, which was a massive relief.

I had turned 18, so now Ani couldn't call me 'kid' any more, and I was free to make my own decisions. I still lived at home, I still looked after my sisters.

Mum was so depressed now, she was making herself ill. It seemed to be getting worse, not better.

Februari had left high school (I had got very emotional because my eldest sister was growing into such a wonderful young lady) and was at college. I missed her like crazy.

March was in Year 10, and was studying for her NLHEs. She had chosen to take History, Mysterian, Music and Geography, and was doing very well.

April was in Year 9 – Options year. This would have been very stressful for her once, but she didn't seem to have a care in the world. She retained a fierce friendship with Mary and Raul Acevedo, who had proved to be two of the nicest children I'd ever met, and their parents were lovely as well.

April had changed so much. She was starting to remind me a lot of myself. She had developed a passion for rock music, which I encouraged. She was very hardworking and modest, and keen to help me in whatever ways she could. The bullying problem had stopped, and my sister was happy.

May was in Year 8, and was very much the same as ever. She loved feeling grown-up, and was constantly going out to meet friends. I was glad to see she was so popular, as I quite clearly hadn't been.

June and July had started high school and still did everything together. They spent their time with another set of twins – Henry and Douglas, who they insisted were just friends (though I heard them giggling in their room more frequently than usual, and couldn't help but wonder if it was anything to do with this).

Augusta was in Year 4, and hadn't changed much either. She still loved art, and frequently came home wielding a new masterpiece. My friends visited often, and out of the rest of my sisters, Augusta became a special favourite of Jemima, who brought her art supplies more often than not.

September was in Year 3, and still longed to be Rapensela when she grew up. Again, she wasn't much different.

Octoba was in Year 2, and was slowly but surely becoming more of her own person.

Little November had started school, and was loving it. She was very interested in learning, and listened to Mr Mills' every word. She was quite clearly the best student in the class, and I was exceptionally proud of her.

December had grown a lot, and had started walking about a year ago. However, she was still the baby of the family despite being a toddler now. She longed to go to school like November, and was now a lot better at talking; the problem now was getting her to be quiet. Nevertheless, I was very proud of her too.

Things had been resolved between Amycus and Sylvia, and I'd persuaded him to give her another chance at friendship. I'd become friends with her too, and I found her a good person to talk to when seeking advice. She was genuinely sorry for all that she had done to Amycus in the past.

When I'd started working at Newgate all that time ago, it had been just after the Easter holidays. So it was almost a year after that when Februari had come into my room on my 18th birthday, which happened to be a Friday.

"Hey, Jan," she said, "are you ready? We're going out, you and me and Mum and the rest of our sisters. You're going to have a really nice time. We got you a dress – look, blue as well, your favourite colour, and matching shoes, and a blue butterfly sparkly clip thingy to go in your hair."

She held out these things. The dress was absolutely stunning.

"Oh, Febs," I whispered, "It's beautiful. Thank you."

"Get changed quickly; we don't want to be late," she said.

"Late for what?"

"You'll see," she said, smiling. So after I changed into the dress – I had to admit, I didn't look quite as average as I normally did... I loved it – we got in the car (Mum was driving and the rest of our sisters were presumably wherever it was we were going) and then after a few minutes, Februari spoke again.

"All right, Jan, close your eyes. We're nearly there." So I closed my eyes, and then I felt the car stop. Februari led me out of the car, and then I walked for a bit with her carefully guiding me, and then she said "Okay... open!" I opened my eyes, and I heard many voices crying, "Happy Birthday, Januari!"

I looked around. We were in the church hall, and practically the whole of Oldgate was there. Certainly everyone I knew. The room was clearly organised for a party – a surprise party. I'd only ever been to one before, Victoria's 18th. I wasn't really much of a people person, but I'd loved it. I turned to Februari.

"*Febs...*" I whispered.

"Don't thank me; it wasn't my idea. It was all Amycus; he organised everything."

I turned around and saw Amycus. I looked at him. "Amycus? You organised all of this?"

"Well, I don't know... Februari and everyone helped... Januari, you look absolutely stunning."

I beamed. Then I walked over to him and hugged him tightly. "Thank you. Thank you so much."

"You're welcome. I... do you like it?"

"Oh, Amycus. I love it. I only have one problem."

"Oh. What is it?" I leaned in and whispered into his ear.

"My boyfriend hates parties." I still struggled calling Amycus my boyfriend. It just didn't seem like the right word. Nevertheless... I was getting used to it, slowly but surely.

"Well... I don't mind, Jan, honestly. I just thought you'd like it. As long as you're happy, I am too."

"Good," I said, satisfied, and after we'd eaten, he came over to me again.

"Now," he said, smiling, "is it too much to ask to want to dance with the most beautiful girl in the room?"

"Of course not," I replied, "Sylvia's right over there, and there's Abigail, Emily, Jemima, Victoria..."

He laughed, "Oh, Jan. You know I'm talking about you."

I smiled, and took his hand. "I've never really been one for dancing."

"Me neither, but perhaps, with you, it will be different."

So I danced with Amycus. The first song was a reasonably slow one, but it was one of my favourites. I must admit, I did quite enjoy dancing slowly in his arms, with my head on his shoulder, my arms around him gently.

"There," he said, smiling, "this isn't so bad, is it?"

"No," I smiled, "but, you know, I know you really don't like parties with lots of people. So if you want to go and get a bit of fresh air at some point, I don't mind."

"Thank you, Januari. You know what this makes me think of? Talking and dancing..."

"Elizabeth Bennet and Mr Darcy?"

"Yes, exactly," he laughed, "Us and our books."

I beamed, and we said nothing more. A little later, he did go outside for a bit. I decided to follow him, hoping no one would notice my absence. I just felt like being alone with him for a bit. I saw him wandering along by the lake. I caught up with him quickly.

"Hello, Amycus," I said.

"Januari? What are you doing out here? It's your party."

"Yeah, well, you're not the only one who likes to have a little breath of fresh air sometimes."

"Okay, okay." He smiled. I wandered along the path beside him. I slipped my hand into his, and we walked in silence, just enjoying each other's company. Eventually, he spoke, "I should hope that this has been one of the best nights of your life."

"Well, I don't know..." I said, grinning. I stopped walking, and turned to face him. We were in the middle of the bridge over the river right by the lake. The moon was directly behind us, and its light was shimmering on the lake. "There's something I still need to do." I leaned up and kissed him softly.

He laughed. "You're still the same Januari," he said, "I was worried that you might have outgrown that silly little fling with Amycus Derby."

"Oh, Amycus. We both know it's more than that. This is love, this is true love. I'll always be your Januari. Besides, you'll always be five years older than me, I can't possibly 'outgrow you'," I teased.

"I always forget the age difference," he said, laughing, "but I'm glad you think that because I'll always be your Amycus. I'll never hurt you. I can't tell you how glad I am that I met you, Januari."

"Well... our first meeting wasn't exactly romantic, was it? I asked you for directions, remember? The first words I spoke to you were 'Excuse me, sir.'"

He laughed. "We haven't changed much, have we?" he said fondly, "and I still can't stop thinking about you. I couldn't take my eyes off you tonight."

"Well... how's this for romance, anyway? Look, the moon is right behind us. Knowing me, I swear this is the point where I try to lean on the edge of the bridge, trip over my own feet and end up falling in the lake."

He laughed again. "You fell out of a tree and landed on me once. You were 11, I was 16. That was actually the first time we met. You said Genevieve dared you to see how far up the tree you could climb. It only came back to me after you saved my life that time. That was when I realised that I really had met a Januari before, I hadn't just imagined it. You probably don't remember."

"Oh, gosh. Was that you? Shoot. Yeah, I remember. Well, that's even less romantic a first meeting."

"I don't mind. You can fall on me whenever you want. I never would have thought that I'd fall in love with you, but I couldn't help it. Sorry."

I laughed, "I love you, Amycus."

"I love you too," He leaned in and kissed me gently. I wrapped my arms around him and pulled him closer.

Then I heard a voice saying, "Awww, you two are so *sweet!*"

I pulled away from him quickly and whirled around. May stood there, in her purpley-pink dress. I flushed.

"May! What are you doing here? How long were you standing there? Wait, no, don't answer that."

"Sorry, I couldn't resist. I followed you from the party. I wanted to see what you were like when you thought you were alone."

"Why?"

"Never mind. Sorry. I'll go now." She scurried off. I turned to Amycus.

"Gosh, there's no privacy, is there?"

"Nope. Why don't we go back now?"

"Okay," I grinned guiltily. "Wow. I wish she hadn't seen that."

"Yeah, me too... oops."

I giggled. "Oops." We headed back to the party, and that was definitely one of the best nights of my life. I felt extremely lucky to have Amycus.

So my life was the happiest I'd ever dreamed it could be, and almost everything was perfect.

I say almost; Amycus had been sort of... distant, lately. He'd been keeping to his classroom instead of spending time with me. When I hadn't seen him for a whole week, I decided things couldn't carry on the way they were going, and went to his classroom to speak to him.

"Amycus?" He quickly turned his computer screen off, and turned to face me.

"Januari. To what do I owe the pleasure?"

"I don't need a reason to come and see you, but, as it happens, there is one. You've been shutting me out lately. You've been spending all your time alone, in here. It's been a week now, and we've barely spoken. I've missed you."

"You know what? You're right. We've barely spoken all week. I've missed you too. I've had a good reason for all this, I assure you. You'll find out soon enough. Until then, I have to just keep doing this."

"Amycus, you can trust me. Whatever it is, you can tell me."

"No, I can't. That would destroy the purpose. You will understand, soon, I promise you."

"If you don't want to spend time with me any more, if you don't feel the same way about me any more... just say so."

He came over to me, and took my hands. "Januari," he said. "I love you. I always have, and I always will. Don't ever think otherwise. It's just... I can't tell you, but I'm doing this for you. Believe me."

"I do believe you, but... I want to spend time with you. Is this something to do with your family?"

"No, nothing to do with that. Liza is... the same as ever. I'm glad I have my sister, but... no one could ever mean as much to me as you do, Jan. You know what? It can't hurt to take one day off. Let's go to the park."

"Really?"

"Yes, I could do with a bit of fresh air. I have missed spending time with you."

"Will you tell me what you've been doing this week?"

He laughed. "Patience, my love. Say no more on the subject, for now. Trust me, it'll be worth the wait. I think you're really going to like it. Just trust me."

"Of course. I won't say anything more, if you don't want me to."

"Good. Come here." He put his arms around me. "I love you, Januari. I would never do anything to hurt you."

"I love you, Amycus."

So then we went to the bench in the park, just like we did in that first half-term. It was just like it used to be. I couldn't help thinking about what it was that Amycus wasn't telling me.

It wasn't like him to keep anything from me, and it made me feel uncomfortable. However, I tried to relax, and just trusted him that he knew what he was doing.

After work, on Friday evening, there was a knock on the door and there he was. I smiled, and invited him in.

"Are you going to tell me what you've been doing this week then?" I asked eagerly. He smiled.

"As promised. You see, the thing is... I have a surprise for you. Your sisters have helped me, and... I think you're going to really like it."

"Okay, now I'm really curious. Remember what happened last time you asked me to close my eyes? That was the happiest moment of my life."

"Me too." He smiled, remembering it. My sisters all came over to me, and gathered around (apart from Februari, obviously, who I've mentioned was at college)

"Can I tell her? Can I? Pleeeease?" begged May.

"All right," replied Amycus.

May turned to me, her eyes shining with excitement. "Jannie," she began "You're going away for the weekend, to Oppidum Leo. With Amycus, and-" March grabbed her arm.

"That's enough, May," she cut in sharply.

"Really? Amycus?" I looked at him. "How long have you been planning this?"

"A while," he informed me. "Only if you want to, of course. I just thought-"

I threw my arms around him. "You're too thoughtful. Thank you. What did I do to deserve you?"

"I love you," he reminded me, "and love is free. Though, as it happens, you've done everything for me. I wanted to do something for you. I know it isn't travelling the world, but... it's a start, I hope."

"Amycus Derby, you are the kindest, most thoughtful person I have ever met. Words cannot explain how much I love you."

He beamed. At that point, April came running downstairs with a big suitcase. "I packed your bag, Jannie. I checked with March, I haven't missed anything. There's a top and your jeans on your bed upstairs for you to change into now."

"Thank you, April. I love you." I turned to Amycus. "I'll just be a minute." He nodded, and I went upstairs.

I couldn't believe he'd really organised all of that for me. I decided I would have to do something to pay him back. I had to do something for him., because he was always doing things for me. He was constantly there for me. He was everything to me, and he always had been.

I changed in a flurry of excitement, and when I went back downstairs, I was almost skipping. I'd never left Lilidell before, let alone Larenia. I was finally going to Oppidum Leo, and I was doing it with my true love. It was so... perfect. Yet some small part of me was screaming that something was bound to go wrong.

That kind of thing just didn't happen to me. I never thought my story would have a happy ending, but now... I wasn't sure. Something could always go wrong, but... I'd found my true love, and that was all I could ever ask for.

I smiled at Amycus.

"Are you ready?" he asked.

I took a deep breath, "yes. I'm ready."

Chapter 30

Likizo

Holiday – Swahili

When we were on the plane, and the flight to Oppidum Leo was about to set off, Amycus took my hand.

"Januari? You're very quiet, which isn't like you at all. Are you nervous?"

I smiled. "No. I'm not nervous. It's just... I've never left the country before, and a few years ago... I never would have dreamed that one day, I'd be sitting here, on a plane to Oppidum Leo with my true love beside me. It really is a dream come true."

"I know how you feel. I wouldn't have thought it either. You are everything I dreamed you'd be and more. You are my dream come true, Januari Winters. All I want is for you to be happy."

"I'm happy when I'm with you, but... can I ask you a question?"

"You just did, but feel free to ask another."

"How is it that you always know exactly what to say and when, and you're always so good at finding beautiful things to say to me?"

He laughed, "I just say what I'm thinking, Jan. Besides, I'm a Larenian teacher, what do you expect? And you say some beautiful things as well."

Then the plane took off. Amycus held my hand tightly, and I smiled. I'd been waiting all my life for a moment like this, and now, it was really happening. I could scarcely believe it.

We sat most of the time in silence, both of us with our heads in books. April had packed my bag very well. She was very compassionate, and very thoughtful, and she knew exactly what I liked. She'd packed me Timeless, Pride and Prejudice and Jane Eyre. She'd also packed the Rosanna and The Sunset Angel. A nice varied range, and she knew how quickly I read books, when I had the time.

When we arrived in Oppidum Leo, we went to the hotel in which we were staying. In the hotel room, there were two single beds, and a small bathroom.

I slept well that night, and my last thoughts before I fell asleep were that I had a whole weekend ahead of me with the man I loved.

When I woke up the next morning, Amycus was sitting on his bed, staring blankly at the wall. I went over to him.

"Good morning, Amycus." He didn't move. "Amycus. Are you all right?"

"Yes, I'm fine. I'm sorry, I was just... thinking. How are you this morning, my Januari?"

"All right. You know, if there's something you want to talk about...?"

"I...Januari, can I ask you a question?"

"Yep."

"I know you never thought any of your dreams would come true. You thought you'd just be living at home until your mid-thirties, and be alone forever, but... things have changed since then, and... well, I've been wondering, what do you expect from your future now?"

This was an extremely difficult question to answer.

"Well, the truth is... I have no idea. Since I met you, and since Father died, I really don't know where my future is going to take me. I still need to look after my sisters. I hope they'll be okay with Mum and March this weekend, but I want to spend time with you too. It surprises me, really, that you still want to be with me, knowing that I have nothing to offer."

"It shouldn't surprise you. I love you. I need you, because you keep me going, and I can always look forward to the next time I'll see you. You're the best person I've ever met, in all factors. You are everything to me, Januari."

"I love you, Amycus," I replied simply, "more than anything."

He smiled and kissed my forehead gently. "Come on, Jannie," he said, standing up, "we have a whole weekend ahead of us, just you and me. Let's not waste it."

I smiled, and hastened to follow him.

As we headed out into Oppidum Leo, Amycus said he didn't mind what we did, but not to go up the Gloria Tower until the next morning.

During the day, we saw everything I'd ever wanted to see in Oppidum Leo. The Temples of Lidia and Carla, the River Leowyq, and the Profunduva Bridge... everything. We looked round the NLAM (National Leonian Art Museum), which Augusta, and Jemima, would have loved.

When we got back to the hotel room that evening, I opened the window. Then I stood and looked out at the night sky. Amycus came to stand beside me.

"It's beautiful, isn't it?" I said quietly. "The night sky. The stars. The moon. Incredible, really."

"Yes, it is," he agreed, "it always used to help me feel calm when I was at the orphanage. I used to think the girl I would fall in love with was looking up at the same night sky, somewhere. The love of my life, and now, she's right next to me."

"I always wanted to travel, and I looked at those stars and saw hope. I used to dream that one day, I'd look up at a different night sky, from a different country, and now not only am I looking up at that night sky, the man I love, the one I thought I'd never find, is standing right beside me."

He smiled. "Januari, I can't help remembering the first time you saved my life, last year. You had me very confused."

I laughed. "In what way?"

"Well, when I was with you, it felt right, but I felt the same way around Janet Woods. I had a dream that my true love would be called Januari. It made sense, if the girl that saved my life was Januari.

But... I couldn't just let go of the way I felt about Janet Woods. Well, you did a very good job of keeping your secret for the first term, because I never would have guessed that Januari and Janet Woods were the same person."

"Well, I apologise for confusing you."

He laughed. "Oh, Januari. I'm glad it worked out like this. I wouldn't have it any other way. Though just before I found out that you were the same person, I'd decided that I couldn't keep waiting for 'Januari' to come along when I was seeing 'Janet' every day, and feeling like this."

"Before I met you, I was afraid of falling in love. I was so convinced that no one would ever think about me like that, I thought I'd only end up with a broken heart."

"At first, I thought you'd never think about me like I thought about you, but when I saw those letters you wrote, and I knew that you trusted me enough to let me read them, and I knew that... you really did love me too."

"I do love you, and there's no one I'd rather have here beside me."

"You are the most important person in my world, Januari. Though I appreciate that isn't saying much."

I grinned. "Goodnight, Amycus. I love you."

"I love you too. Goodnight, Januari."

That night, as I lay in the bed nearest to the window, I thought that I'd better make the most of the next day, because I'd be going home the next afternoon.

Chapter 31

Ar cheann de na chiumhneacháin happiest de mo shaol

One of the happiest moments of my life – Irish

The next morning, we went to the Gloria Tower. We got there nice and early (It opened at 9am) so there weren't many people there.

We went right up to the top, and I gazed out. The sky was very clear, and there was city as far as the eye could see.

"Look, Amycus, you can see for miles," I said. He smiled, and came over to stand beside me.

"It's breathtaking, isn't it?" he said pensively. I nodded, speechless. He took my hands, and I turned to face him. "Jan, there's something I've been meaning to ask you."

"Anything."

He took a deep breath, "Januari Snow Winters," he began, "would you do me the honour of being my wife?"

I stared at him, unable to reply. So he continued, "if you don't feel ready, I'm not forcing you to do anything, but... we've been through so much together, and... I have loved you almost from the moment we met. You are the one I want to spend the rest of my life with. I don't want to put any pressure on you, but... I think it's time to start living our happy ending."

"Oh, Amycus. This means so much to me, but I'm thinking of my sisters... I still have to look after them, and I don't think Mum-"

"Januari. For once in your life, stop thinking of other people. Forget about everything else, and tell me – what do *you* want?"

I hesitated, then replied, "I want to spend the rest of my life with you. If I married you, then I would live happily ever after. I want nothing more. That's what I want, when I only think of me, but in reality, there isn't only me. There are my sisters, and Mum, and my friends, and you, and... I don't know what to do."

"I... you know your sisters helped me plan this weekend, don't you? Februari wrote you this, last time she visited. Here." He pulled out a piece of paper with Februari's handwriting on it, and it said as follows.

Dear Jannie,

When you go to Oppidum Leo, and Amycus Derby asks you to marry him, don't think of us. Think of yourself, and what you want.

We all want you to be happy, and we know you love him. This is your chance to live happily ever after, and you can't give it up for our sake.

If you say yes, Mum can look after us, and I can help her. I think it would be good for Mum to be forced to look after her own children. It's about time she thought about us, as well as herself.

We discussed this with her, and she agreed that she's been unfair to you, and that your family shouldn't keep you from your happy ending.

Think about it, and make a decision based on your own choices, and what you want. We know you'll do the right thing – you always do.

Lots of love,

Februari, March, April, May, June, July, Augusta, September, Octoba, November and December ♥

I looked up, and made a decision. Amycus looked at me.

"What did they say, Jan?"

"They told me not to let them keep me from my happy ending, and that they knew I would do the right thing."

"So... will you marry me?"

"Yes."

I threw my arms around him. He laughed. "I love you, Januari Winters. No matter what happens, and I always will."

"I love you, Amycus Derby. I always have and I always will."

"It's like you said: I'm not alone and I'm not unloved."

"You remembered my exact words? From a year ago?"

"I remember everything you say."

"Well... I'd better be careful what I say, then."

He grinned. Then he kissed me, and I knew that my happy ending was just around the corner. It was no longer a dream, it was my future.

So then he slid a ring onto my finger, beaming. He told me that I was going to make all his dreams come true.

He was making my dreams come true, all at once. Except that I no longer cared about travelling. I didn't care where I went as long as it was with Amycus.

I knew that my sisters were right – I had made the right choice. I had everything I'd ever wanted right by my side.

We went back to the hotel then, and packed our things ready to go. I couldn't believe the weekend in Oppidum Leo was over already.

This had been one of the happiest moments of my life. Not the happiest, that had been when Amycus kissed me for the first time, and the first time I heard him tell me he loved me, and I could freely tell him how I really felt. I loved Amycus, and that would never change.

Epilogue

No more drama

Les lletres
The letters – Catalan

It was that kind of feeling where I was so happy that nothing else mattered in the world. Where I was really, truly happy.

On the plane home, Amycus took some sheets of paper out of his bag.

"Januari," he said "These were some letters I wrote at different points in my life. I found them in my sideboard drawer the other day, and I'd like you to read them."

"Are you sure?"

"You trusted me with your letters to your father. Now I'll trust you with mine, to... no one in particular. I can't even remember."

I smiled, and turned my eyes to the letters.

The first of Amycus' letters was as follows:

Dear no one,

I am writing this to no one because there is no one I can trust enough to tell them this. I have no family, and no friends.

I feel as if I can confide in this piece of paper more than any person. I want to record some... things. My dream is to find my true love. I was told in a dream that her name would be Januari.

It's a very pretty name, and quite unusual. I'm sure I will know when I meet her, because no one else is nice to me. I just want someone who is kind, and intelligent, and brave, and who understands me, and doesn't judge me when they meet me.

In the dream, it said she would find me, so that means I just have to... wait? All I want is to find someone who cares, because there must be some decent people out there. Somewhere. This world can't be all dark... can it?

Sincerely,

Amycus Derby, age 11

I didn't know what to make of that. When this was written, I would have been only six. Still happy, before anything changed. Just in my second year of junior school, with not a care in the world. The man who I would fall in love with was achingly close by, only in Newgate, and was feeling alone, and unloved. Yet he still had hope. I read on:

Dear no one,

I can't believe how stupid I was that I actually believed my dream was real, that it meant something.

I still want to be loved, and to know someone I can love, but I know that won't happen. No one would love me, the boy I've turned out to be.

I might as well just forget about it, but I can't. It's just a dream that will never come true. I'm not even me any more, I'm just Friendless. My dream is all I have left, and it will never come true.

I had a girlfriend, called Sylvia, and she meant so much to me, we were friends for years, and then... she was my girlfriend, but then I saw her kissing Jake, and she told me she was never even my friend; she just wanted to see how close she could get to me. I don't even feel like I can trust anyone any more, not that I could in the first place.

So I don't know what I'm going to do with my life. Every living moment is going to be completely pointless. I feel as if I'm falling apart, I'm not even a person any more. I'm just a broken, mentally scarred, depressed, friendless shadow.

Sometimes I wonder why I even bother.

Sincerely,

Amycus Derby, age 15

I almost cried reading this. This was someone I loved, and he was so sad. He almost always meant what he said, which meant he really believed all this. I looked at him. "Oh, Amycus."

He glanced at the paper. "Ah. Yes. I was completely despairing at that age. I don't deny it, I must have been an awful person to be around. I was still like that when I met you. You brought the real me back to the surface. The only way to describe me as a teenager is... lost."

"What was Sylvia like when you knew her?"

"She was... very kind, and thoughtful, and she was so... sweet. At least, I thought she was, but it turns out we were never even real friends. It was a trick right from the beginning, and it still hurts remembering."

"I'm so sorry," I took his hand.

"Don't be," he said, "it's the past now."

"I wish I could have done something, if I'd only known..."

"Januari, you have done something. You were the only one who ever bothered to do something. Anyway, it gets better... read on."

I turned to the next letter, almost afraid to read what he wrote.

Dear no one,

I am now a Larenian teacher at Newgate High School. I should be grateful, I suppose; it is a job well-suited to me. I have my own house now, and... this is probably what I'll be doing for the rest of my life, so I'd better get used to it.

None of my colleagues are very nice, and they talk about me behind my back, but then again, that's all people ever do. I still think of what I once dreamed of, and often, but I do not realistically expect it to come true.

My attitude from when I was 15 is unchanged. I wish more than anything that I could meet my soulmate, my true love, but I cannot imagine that happening.

Oh, Januari, where are you? Why have you not come into my life? I know I am still young, and I have my entire life ahead of me, but I need you now more than ever. My life is a misery, and without love, there is no point to my existence. I doubt anyone would care if I ceased to exist. I only wish I could find Januari, because I am sick of waiting.

Sincerely,

Amycus Derby, Age 20

I couldn't believe he'd been so... depressed. He'd lived so close by, yet until last year, we'd never met. I looked at Amycus now.

"I'm sorry," he said, "reading these must be really depressing. It does get better, I promise you."

I smiled. "I just... I can't believe we never met before last year. We were living so close by..."

"It's because I was antisocial. Everyone in Oldgate knows Januari Winters, and there'd been plenty of trips to Oldgate, but I'd never bothered going. I wish we had met sooner."

"I think you were really brave, keeping going through all that."

"Oh, Jannie. I'm the opposite of brave. I'm glad you think that, but..."

"Amycus. Stop it. You always put yourself down, and you shouldn't. You're a good person."

"Thank you, Januari. Why don't you keep reading now?"

I nodded, and started to read the next letter.

Dear no one,

The day before yesterday I met someone called Janet Woods, and she's only a year younger than me. She is unlike any other person I've met. She is kind, and she doesn't judge me.

Now, she's my friend. Finally, someone I can talk to, someone who isn't like all the other people, who isn't cruel, who doesn't hate me.

It may not be true love, but it's the next best thing. When I first met her, I thought she might be Januari, and for a second, I dared to hope, and then she told me her name was Janet Woods. I don't think I'll ever find love but at least, in the meantime, I have a friend. For the first time in my life, I feel less alone.

Sincerely,

Amycus Derby, age 22

I was extremely glad for the change of tone, and I then proceeded straight to the next letter.

Dear no one,

Yesterday, I went to the park with Janet, and today, she got me to smile. That would be the first time in ten years, and I'm actually feeling passionate emotions again.

Then she hugged me. No one has ever hugged me before. I felt exceedingly strange. I assume this is what it feels like, having friends, but I feel so lucky to have met her. I actually don't mind that I haven't found my true love and probably never will, because I have a friend, and that in itself was life-changing. For me, anyway.

Sincerely,

Amycus Derby, age 22

I laughed. I remembered how it had felt when I'd hugged him that time. I hadn't meant to, of course, but it had been a real milestone, seeing him smile for the first time.

Dear no one,

Today, I told Janet to call me Amycus, not Mr Derby. Because then it really feels like she's my friend, and I feel even less alone.

Yesterday, she said she's keeping something from me. Something big, but I don't particularly care, to be completely honest. As long as this is the real her, the person I know. She seems convinced that she's a bad person, but I know her, and I know that she isn't.

Janet Woods is a good person. The sweetest girl I've ever met, but I'm worried… I'm starting to feel really different around her. Strange. I think I might be falling in love with her.

She's so kind, and intelligent, and I want to get to know her better, but she isn't my true love. She can't be. Unless… it really was just a dream. A meaningless dream, because when I'm with Janet, I'm happy. Really happy. I'm just going to have to see what happens from this point onwards.

Sincerely,

Amycus Derby, age 22

He'd been a lot more willing to admit his feelings to himself than I had. I hadn't even considered that possibility until I realised it for definite. Smiling to myself, I turned my eyes to the next letter.

Dear no one,

Yesterday, I saw Janet, and I met her sister. Her sister's name is Februari. Janet kissed me on the cheek. It made me realise – it's not every day I meet a girl like that.

And… I really think I do love her, but there's nothing I can do about it. She's one in a million; what can I say?

But then something else happened, in the early hours of this morning. I was with all the people from the orphanage, last night. They've changed, they're half-decent now. Or, at least, Benjamin, Abigail and her friend Emily seem nice. Jake is the same as ever.

And Jake was with some other guys, and he was drunk, and he tried to kill me, and then someone saved me. She was brave, and she said her name was Januari. It felt right when I was with her, but it's the same feeling when I'm with Janet. I don't know what to do.

She said I would see her again, but wouldn't know it was her. I have no idea what that means. It gets weirder – I accidentally called Janet "Januari" last night, because I was thinking about that dream, and she didn't notice. What on Somnium is going on here? My life has been turned upside down. I have no idea how this is going to work out. This is not what I thought love would be like.

Sincerely,

Amycus Derby, age 22

So we'd realised our feelings for one another in that same moment. Part of me wished I'd acted on them then, but then again I liked things the way they'd happened.

Dear no one,

Nothing has changed much, but today, Janet was upset. She was crying, and I knew there must be something badly wrong, because Janet is brave, and Brian – damn him – told me it would be best to stay away from her.

But I know that different people need different things when they are upset. I like to be left alone, but I am quite sure Janet at least wants someone to take her mind off whatever is bothering her. So she came with me to my classroom, and we talked.

I don't want to confide what she was upset about to a piece of paper, but... I feel as if there is a lot more to her than meets the eye. That her secret might be something that affects her hugely.

Either way, I ended up keeping an eye on one of her sisters – May – for her, while she taught a lesson and I had a free period. May seemed a very nice girl though very... sociable. She showed me a book, which was written by another of her sisters.

It was very well-written. And the story... well, it got to me. It was about two friends called Markos and Janey who were in love, but didn't realise it. Then Janey lost everything, and had to move to the other side of the world, and they married people they didn't love and never saw each other again.

It made me realise – I will, at some point, have to tell Janet how I feel about her. No matter what her secret is, it can't change the way I feel. Nothing can. I can't stop thinking about her.

I can't keep waiting for some character from a dream to come along, even if she did save my life.

Because when I'm with Janet Woods, the moments are golden. There is no one like her.

Sincerely,

Amycus Derby, age 22

He'd changed so much from that boy he'd been when he wrote that first letter. The things he'd said about me were really touching, and I glanced at him for a moment, speechless, then looked back to the letters to see that this next one was the last.

Dear no one,

I see no point in writing letters to no one any more, because I have found my true love.

It turns out Jan's secret is that she isn't Janet Woods at all. She is a 17-year-old called Januari Winters. She lied because she needed the job, and she wanted to create a better life for her family.

She has 11 sisters, and she has to look after them because her father is ill and her mother is depressed. She's given up everything for them, and that is bravery. That is determination, and that is love. I admire her for it. She has done this since she was ten as well. Quite unbelievable.

It was her who saved my life last week, and she loves me. She told me that she loves me. This is everything I'd ever dreamed of. She is my dream come true, literally. So this will be the last letter addressed to no one, because I now have someone I can really trust, and confide in. She has turned my life around, and now I feel as if I have a purpose. There is a reason for everything, and Januari Snow Winters is everything to me.

Sincerely,

Amycus Derby, age 22

I looked at him. "I meant every word of it," he said quietly.

"I know you did," I replied, "as did I, when I wrote my letters. I... that means a lot, Amycus. I had no idea... that I could even affect someone's life that much."

"You changed my life forever, Januari Winters. You really have done everything for me. I don't know what I did to deserve you. You're one in a million, Jannie."

I leaned across and kissed him passionately, and I knew that this was everything I'd ever wanted.

Ua noho maikaʻi lākou ma hope
And they lived happily ever after – Hawaiian

So throughout my life, most people lived happily ever after.

Februari became a famous actress, and made lots of money. The best part is, Alfie Barker came crawling back to her, telling her he was sorry, and he wanted to be with her after all. Februari told him to go and... well, you get the picture. She married a man who made her happy, and who had known her since before she started acting.

March became a bestselling author, and dedicated her first book to me, which was very touching.

She wrote some fantasy books, full of magical beings that she had invented herself. She also wrote some books based on reality. People that seemed real.

Some of the stories were based on stories she'd come up with as a little girl, or as a teenager. She published the story of Markos and Janey, and countless others that I remember from different points in her childhood.

April became a music teacher. When she was older, she married Raul Acevedo. On their wedding night, I remember her telling me that it was me who'd helped to stop her from being depressed.

She told me that "Meeting new friends is important in bringing light to people's lives but when the fire is burning, you realise that the most vital part was the one you took for granted, who was there for you the whole time."

She was a very good music teacher, and she actually taught December and November for a brief period while they were at high school.

She and Raul were happy together, and they saw Raul's sister Mary very often. Mary lived nearby as well, so they saw each other most days.

May became an actress, like Februari. They starred in films together, and both made me very proud. May married a man with red hair, who she thought was very good-looking, and I have to admit, they really are soulmates, both very social, neither able to be quiet for more than five minutes at a time. Definitely made for each other. So May makes lots of money and lives happily with her husband.

June became a PE teacher. She was never one for romance, but she still found a man who could sweep her off her feet. She loves him, I can tell, even if she won't admit it. I'm sure her happily ever after ending is going to involve him somehow.

He is a footballer, who is growing in fame, and June often joins him when he practises. By his invitation, of course. They often spend time together.

July started working in the local hairdresser's, and the job couldn't be more suited to her. She also trained in other things in the salon, such as nails and make-up. So she's basically a stylist.

She and June still see each other every day. They sometimes come round to visit me, and sometimes they do things alone together, just June and July. 'Twin time,' they call it. They haven't changed much.

Augusta became an artist, as did Jemima. They both did the same job – selling their own artwork. They've also been teaching art to supplement their incomes.

Augusta's style is more cartoon-like, and she loves drawing characters, people. Whereas Jemima's artistic style is more realistic, as it always was. I have paintings by both of them.

September has been working in the nursery for a year, with Ani, and helping to look after the young children. She's only an assistant at the moment, but she gets a small amount of money for doing it, and wants to study childcare further.

Octoba is still at school, and is doing very well with all her work. November and December are also still at school, and are quite the couple of teenagers now. Both very grown-up, I can scarcely believe it.

I'm very proud of all my sisters. Jemima, Victoria and Genevieve all achieved their dreams from when we were children. Jemima you already know about, Victoria is a professional translator and Genevieve an astrophysicist. Victoria also married Luciano, the Mysterian boy.

Amycus' sister Liza told us all about his past: Their mother Susan's boyfriend had got her pregnant when she was just 16. Then he'd left her, and moved away.

She'd been prepared to take on the task of raising a child, but not two. So when she gave birth to twins, a boy and a girl, she took the girl – Liza – home with her and abandoned the boy on the street with the following note:

To whom it may concern,

This child's name is Amycus Charles Derby. When found, he should be taken to an orphanage, and when old enough, should be told his parents are dead, and that he has no siblings. I will not tell you otherwise.

Liza discovered this when she was ten, and was so disgusted at what her mother had done that she ran away from home and found her Father. Liza and her father had been searching for Amycus ever since, but never found him until by sheer coincidence, Susie had another heart attack following the car crash and she died shortly afterwards. Amycus and Liza's father was dead too, as Amycus already knew.

Liza now lived in Lilidell too, and worked as a journalist for the local newspaper. She was very good at writing things factually, and was a very logical sort of person.

Jake Barker was arrested for being found in possession of illegal drugs. Alfie Barker seemed to be going the same way.

I have no idea what became of Ella Wright, but I know what happened to the people from the orphanage where Amycus grew up; Benjamin continued to work in the supermarket and two of the girls whom he'd mentioned before – Abigail and Emily – worked in the same hairdresser's as July.

And what of me? I married Amycus when I was 19. That was when Mum finally got over her depression. She got a new job working as a receptionist/telephonist at the doctor's, which she enjoyed a lot. Before that, we'd been living off a pitifully small sum of money provided by life insurance when my father was diagnosed.

She started spending time with my sisters, and she was happy again, and so was I. Amycus and I both continued to work at Newgate High School.

I remember, on our wedding night, as I stood gazing out at the stars, Amycus came and stood beside me.

"So," he said, "Is this a happy enough ending for you, Mrs Derby? Because if this was a story, it would just end here."

"Not an ending," I replied, "this is a whole new beginning. It might be where the story ends, but it's where the sequel starts. I have a feeling we're going to live happily ever after."

"Wise words, as always." He grinned. "For the happiest moments of my life, I'd say this is second. Of course, nothing can beat the first time you told me you loved me. How does it feel being Januari Derby?"

"Good," I grinned back at him, "oh, and Amycus... I told you so."

He laughed. "I knew you were going to say that. You said you would, a few weeks after we met, and I said I'd never forget you."

"Yeah... I just never thought that your happily ever after would involve me."

"Life is full of surprises. However, I knew that if I had a happy ending, it would involve you. I just never thought I would get a happy ending, but I'm glad things worked out like this."

"Me too. I still don't know what the future holds, but I think I'm going to like it."

"Yep. I'll try and be a good prince charming for you, my princess."

"No. I don't want a prince charming. I'd much rather have Amycus Derby, and... princess? Really?"

"Yes. Seeing as we're married now, I can give you whatever nickname I want, gorgeous."

I gave him a shove. "Oh, not this again, honey."

"Yes, this again, angel."

"Oh, stop it, darling."

"But I don't feel like stopping yet, precious."

I laughed. "We have some weird conversations sometimes, and you definitely started it this time."

"Yes. I guess I did. Just let's not get started on calling each other 'baby'."

I flinched. "Gosh, no!"

He laughed, "I can't believe what's happened today. It's like a dream."

"But it isn't," I replied, "it's real. Or are you still wondering whether I'm real or not?"

"Oh, don't bring that up again," he said, and I grinned.

So this may be the final page of the final chapter, but don't think of it as a happy ending. Think of it as a new beginning. The story ends here because there's nothing more to say. No more drama, just a quiet life for me.

So I guess it turned out well after all. I couldn't have predicted that my life would lead me here. I never thought I'd find someone like Amycus. I never imagined myself getting married, but this is the way things happened, and my story continues.

The story ends here, but my life still goes on, and there's no other way to phrase it: We lived happily ever after.

About the novel

I came up with the original idea for Fire and Ice when I was sitting in my room one day, teaching myself German. I'd just learnt the names of all the months, and had them written down on a piece of paper, and was repeating them over and over to myself.

I suddenly had the thought – *what if there were a couple that had 12 children, all named after the months of the year?* Right from the beginning, Januari was my main character. I knew exactly what she was going to be like, the oldest of all the twelve. Her sisters came next, and the plotline developed slowly.

Amycus Derby didn't come in until a lot later. He came in when I knew she was going to lie in order to get a job as a teacher. The first person she met was the very serious Larenian teacher who at first was only another minor character, but it appears that in my mind, Amycus and Januari just couldn't stay away from each other, and Amycus soon became the character he is.

I knew as soon as I had developed the character that his name would be Amycus. As they teased him in the orphanage, the boy whose name meant "friend" but had none.

The surname was more difficult. I came up with his last name when in the car on the way back from a holiday in Cornwall. I was thinking to myself: *What should his last name be? Well, the author of my favourite book series got some of hers from maps...* and a short while later, we passed a road sign saying "Derby – 30 miles" and I thought maybe that would work, so I tried it out: *Amycus Derby*, and it seemed to work, so from then on, that was his last name.

Amycus became more and more of an important character until eventually, I decided to write a novel with him as the main character.

So Fire and Ice may be over, but my next book will be Forever Alone – which is the same story, but from Amycus' point of view.

Thank you for reading my novel, which was completed Tuesday 27th December 2016. I hope you enjoyed it and I hope that it won't be too long until I begin publishing my next novel!

Please sign up to my newsletter, review my book and read more about my work on

www.ElizabethEBurdon.com

Elizabeth E. Burdon

Elizabeth is student currently at high school, and has wanted to be an author since she was seven years old. That was when she first read the Harry Potter series. She is a keen reader and a very determined writer. She has also written three of her own songs. Her real passion, however, is taking the many ideas in her head and making them into stories which she can tell. She has now written six novels and is currently working on a seventh. No matter what happens, she will never stop telling her stories.

October 2017

A note – If you have a dream, you should never let it go because dreams can come true, through perseverance, hope, and a refusal to give up.

28729919R00162

Printed in Great Britain
by Amazon